THE CHERRY VALLEY MIDDLE SCH

.cherry

DEAR KNOW-IT-ALL

★   ★   ★

Everyone's a Critic

by RACHEL WISE

Simon Spotlight

New York   London   Toronto   Sydney   New Delhi

SIMON SPOTLIGHT
An imprint of Simon & Schuster Children's Publishing Division
1230 Avenue of the Americas, New York, New York 10020
Copyright © 2013 by Simon & Schuster, Inc. All rights reserved, including the right of reproduction in whole or in part in any form.
SIMON SPOTLIGHT and colophon are registered trademarks of Simon & Schuster, Inc.
Text by Veera Hiranandani
Designed by Bob Steimle

For information about special discounts for bulk purchases, please contact Simon & Schuster Special Sales at 1-866-506-1949 or business@simonandschuster.com.
Manufactured in the United States of America 1112 OFF
First Edition 10 9 8 7 6 5 4 3 2 1
ISBN 978-1-4424-6820-7 (pbk)
ISBN 978-1-4424-6821-4 (hc)
ISBN 978-1-4424-6822-1 (eBook)
Library of Congress Control Number 2012950925

Chapter 1

NEWSPAPER STAFF PLAYS MUSICAL CHAIRS. EVERYONE LOSES!

Have you ever wished you knew everything? My name is Samantha Martone and I'll tell you a little secret. I'm supposed know everything, at least once a week.

It's a little funny that I write a column for my middle school newspaper, the *Cherry Valley Voice*, called Dear Know-It-All, where I'm supposed to act like I know everything, which I don't.

Here's another secret: I can't tell anyone I write the column—not my annoying older sister, Allie, who's always getting into my business, and not even my BFF, Hailey Jones. But those are the rules, and if I want to be editor in chief of the paper next year, I've got to stick to them.

Sometimes people write in about boy problems. What do I know about boys, anyway? They remain a constant mystery to me. My forever crush, Michael Lawrence, who I've known since kindergarten and who still calls me Pasty just because I decided to sample an itsy-bitsy taste of paste once when I was five, still hasn't asked me out, at least I don't think so. I haven't asked him out either. At least I'm pretty sure. Hailey says that when I asked him over to work on a story, that was asking him out, but I'm not really sure. This year we've been closer than ever, since Mr. Trigg, our newspaper advisor, puts us together on big investigative stories all the time. Michael will call me or I'll call him to get together for *Voice* stuff, but then the story we're working on tends to complicate things and I end up getting confused. Are we just cowriters, or are we friends, or possibly more than that? It's hard balancing two things I love: being a good investigative reporter and Michael Lawrence.

Trigger, or Mr. Trigg to the general public, says that it's a reporter's job to keep an open mind. It's our job to be good listeners and find out the real facts. It's not our job to know everything. We present the facts and the reader makes up his or her mind. So if I don't actually have to know anything, then I guess I'm doing a great job!

This is what I have to put up with as far as not knowing how to read Michael Lawrence. Today I was late for the meeting we always have after the *Voice* comes out to review the issue. Usually I'm one of the first people there, and I tried to save Michael a seat. But I was having one of those days—you know those days when nothing goes right?

First I slept past my alarm. Then Allie, who truly does think she knows everything, took back the green hoodie I was going to wear (after *she* was the one who gave it to me and told me how good it looked with my long reddish-brown hair!). Then, when I got to school, Hailey seemed annoyed. Our lockers are right near each other, and she was unloading her backpack. She gave me a quick glance and looked away. Hailey always looks great in a natural, sporty way. She's forever tan because she spends so much time outside playing sports and running around. Honestly, she'd look cute in a garbage bag. Today she had on a turquoise-and-white-striped long-sleeved T-shirt that looked great with her blue eyes. I glanced down at the old stretched-out purple sweater I was wearing and sighed. It was the only thing I could find that was somewhat clean after Allie raided my room.

"Um, hello?" I said.

"Hi," she said without looking at me, and went back to digging in the depths of her locker.

"Are you mad at me?" I asked, my heart beating a little faster. I hated when Hailey was mad at me, which she hardly ever was. If she was, she usually had a good reason.

She finally looked at me. "It's just that . . ." And then she stopped.

"What?" I said.

"Oh, Sammy, it's just that I feel like you're so wrapped up in other things—the *Voice*, Michael, your schoolwork—and we don't have enough time to hang out. And I'm always the one e-mailing or calling *you*. I feel like I need to make an appointment just to talk to you lately."

"Sorry, Hails," I said, my stomach feeling kind of grumbly. I didn't have time to eat breakfast. "You got me. I *have* been swamped. But I'll do better. Double promise."

"Okay. Or else I just might have to find a new bestie," she said, her eyes twinkling. With that, she side-kicked me in the butt. That's the great thing about Hailey. She doesn't hold grudges. I side-kicked her back and we were on our way to first period. One problem solved. I made a note in my notebook: *Call Hailey tonight*. She was right. I needed to make more time for her, and I felt kind of bad about it.

The rest of the day wasn't too bad, but at the end of the day, while I was rushing to make the *Voice* meeting, I tripped on some invisible bump in the floor and my notebook, where I keep all my lists and notes for the paper, came flying out of my bag. Seriously, this day needed to end. I knelt down to pick it up and two sneakered feet stopped right in front of me.

"Hey, Trippy! Need a hand?" Ah, another nickname—just what I needed. Michael Lawrence is always coming up with ridiculous new nicknames for me. "Pet names," as Hailey calls them. Maybe they were, but they just felt annoying most of the time, especially right now. I looked up and there he was, flashing his baby blues at me, holding out a hand. He must have seen me trip, and it's not the first time he's witnessed my klutziness. My cheeks went hot. How come I always trip in front of him and not in front of Hailey?

"That's okay, Mikey." I got up and dusted myself off. "They really should fix that!" I said, glaring at the spot on the floor where I'd tripped. Michael looked where I was looking.

"Yeah, you really gotta watch out for those dangerous flat floors," he said with a grin. "You okay?"

"Just fine; let's go. We're late," I said, trying to ignore the cute smirk on his face. We rushed off and burst into the newsroom. It was full and we had to stand in the back, which is why I'm usually always early.

"It's a tad loud in here. Listen up, fellow journos!" bellowed Mr. Trigg, clapping his hands. The room quieted down.

"Okay, the *Voice* is doing great this year, but we don't want to get stale. Writers must stay on their toes to keep it fresh. That's why we're all going to stretch our comfort zones for this issue and do a little switcheroo."

Now you could hear a pin drop. Michael nudged me and raised his eyebrows. I just shrugged.

"So for the next issue, the news reporters are going to covers arts, the sportswriters are going to tackle the news, and the arts reporters are going to do sports. Clear?"

Arts? Was he serious? I mean, I love plays and movies and books and all that. But what really gets me excited about writing for the paper is getting the unexpected story. We've covered things like the new school curriculum; our school's possible Pay for Play program, where kids will have to pay to play after-school sports; and why the cafeteria food is, or *was*, so bad. In all these cases, we unearthed a story that not only surprised us and made people think, but also usually created change for the better. No offense to the arts reporters, but writing a movie review isn't the same. Then a headline popped into my head, as they often do: *Newspaper Staff Plays Musical Chairs. Everyone Loses!*

The editor in chief, Susannah Johnson, raised her hand. "Mr. Trigg, I'm not sure this is going to work. The reporters have all worked hard to develop their beats. We could end up with one of the worst issues of all time!" Lots of people murmured to one another and nodded. Michael let out a "Here, here!" This time I nudged him.

"Winston Churchill said during World War Two, 'I never worry about action, only inaction!'" Mr. Trigg proclaimed. "Trust me, folks, this challenge will make you better reporters. Now let's shuffle around the assignments; we don't have much more time."

Mr. Trigg, who's British and obsessed with World War II, always finds a reason to throw in a Winston Churchill quote. After he gave out a bunch of assignments, he called on me and Michael.

"Okay, Lawrence and Martone, investigative reporters extraordinaire, this time you guys are going to 'investigate' the school play and review it. Since it won't be performed for a couple of weeks, you'll both take a break this week to think about your new roles on the arts beat."

I wasn't sure I wanted a break. A break meant that Michael and I would spend a lot less time together, which added more points to the "against" column of Mr. Trigg's crazy idea.

Ugh. I thought for a second. Well, maybe it would be a good thing. I would only have to write the Dear Know-It-All column for the upcoming issue instead of a news story as well, and that would mean I could spend more time with Hailey.

Michael and I walked back to our lockers together. I kept stealing glances at him. He was wearing my favorite outfit of his, a blue-and-white collared shirt with the sleeves rolled up and jeans. I could see his strong tan arms. He looked at me, and I looked down fast.

"So what do you think of the new arrangement,

Paste?" he asked. "Maybe Trigger has really lost it this time."

"Well, I'm thinking of it as a little vacation," I said, smiling, trying to be positive.

"A vacation from me?" he said, suddenly going all puppy dog on me.

My face fell. "No, of course not, I just meant—"

"I'm just messing with you, Trippy," he said, and gave my ponytail a tug. "See ya. Gotta get to practice!"

I watched as he turned left and walked down the hallway to his locker. He ran into Frank, the quarterback who's on the football team with him. They gave each other a high five and continued on.

I realized I was just standing there, blatantly staring. I forced myself to hustle straight ahead to my locker. Boys. If I ever figure out Michael Lawrence, then maybe I *will* actually know it all.

Chapter 2

GIRL SAVES BEST FRIEND FROM LOSING CRUSH!

★ ★ ★

"What do you think you're doing?" Allie said, marching into her room with her head down, fingers flying on her phone, texting.

"How can you even see me with your head buried in your phone like that?" I asked, trying to distract her since she just caught me raiding her closet for something cute to wear tomorrow. Allie's the neat one, and actually bothers to fold all her clothes on her shelves and in the drawers. I have to remember to put back everything as it was. Allie will notice if just one tiny thing is different from how she left it. She'd probably make a great detective.

"I'm going to get a padlock," she said, finally looking up at me.

"I thought you had play practice." I said.

"Oh, so this is what you do when I'm not around—steal my clothes? Trying to figure out what to wear to impress Mr. Crush? Get out," she said, flinging herself on her bed. She went back to answering her text, paused for a second to check out her sparkly blue manicure, then continued poking at her phone.

Since Allie started rehearsals for the school play, her inner diva, which was already sort of there, has been fully unleashed. She has one of the big supporting roles in *West Side Story*, but you would think she'd been nominated for an Academy Award. I'll admit, the school play is a really big deal in my town. The middle school joins together with the high school to put on a huge production. The sets take almost a year to make. People from all over the town, not just family and friends, come to it. It's an amazing opportunity for the middle school kids too. They rarely get leads, but they do get some of the parts and play a major role on the stage crew. Our drama club always wins lots of awards, regionally and even nationally. But this doesn't mean Allie can walk around like she's the next Selena Gomez. At least not at home.

"Fine, I'll go. I'm sorry," I said, hanging my head and trying to look hopeless. Allie may be a diva, but she has a soft spot for helping me.

"Oh, all right," she said, looking up. "I'll let you borrow one thing."

She bought it. ***Potential Thief Fakes Hurt Feelings and Scores!*** I felt a little bad, but she did take away the one shirt she actually said I could wear before I even got a chance to wear it.

"The green shirt?"

"You can wear it tomorrow, promise," she said, and then she was back with her phone.

I went into the den. I needed to call Hailey ASAP. I wanted her to get a call from me the moment she got home from soccer practice. I settled into the big leather armchair and dialed.

"Hey, how was practice?" I asked when Hailey

answered. My stomach started making noises. Suddenly, I realized how starving I was. I seem to need to eat all the time, and I get really grumpy when I'm hungry—another lovely fact about me that Michael knows, since he's heard my stomach during *Voice* meetings. No wonder he hasn't actually asked me out.

"Whoa, a phone call from Samantha Martone! Where's the fire?"

"Okay, okay, I know I deserved that, but we've moved on, right?"

"Right, right," Hailey said.

I brought the cordless with me into the kitchen and started rummaging for food. I found a bag of cashew nuts and started chomping away.

"Are you eating?" Hailey asked. "Or rather, what are you eating?"

"Cashew nuts."

"Why would you eat those when you have so many better choices?" she asked. Hailey is really picky. She probably eats about ten foods and wishes that high-fructose corn syrup was a food group. Her mom cooks superhealthy stuff all the time—like tofu veggie stir-fries and lentil burgers. She thinks our regular dinners, like chicken with mashed potatoes and gravy, are the bomb. She considers pretzels junk food. I, on the other hand, need lots of different foods to keep my tummy happy.

"I like cashews."

"Okay, so can I come over tomorrow?"

"Sure. Actually, you could come over every day this week! I found out that I don't have to write an article for the next paper, except—," I said, and stopped myself.

"Except what?" she asked.

I took some time to chew a big handful of cashews and gather my thoughts.

"Except (chew), um (chew, chew), that . . . once again, I won't see Michael as much." Wow, that was crazy close. I almost said "except the Dear Know-It-All column." It's not easy to keep one of the biggest things going on in your life from your best friend. You know how a wet paint sign makes you want to touch the paint? Well, sometimes, just because I can't say the name of the column, it's always on the tip of my tongue. "But I'll get to see you more. You'll be sick of me by the end of the week."

"Sick of you? Never. But I'm kind of getting sick of the sound of cashew nuts being chewed in my ear."

"Sorry," I said over a big mouthful.

"Okay, enjoy your snack. See you tomorrow!"

I got off the phone with Hailey, went to my room, and logged in online. I scanned my favorite news Websites and our local town newspaper blog. I always keep up with the town news. Allie was still in her room, blasting music, and my mom was in her home office. It was a perfect time to look through the latest Dear Know-It-All letters that I had shoved into my pocket. I fished them out and read them. As usual, there were some goofy ones like *"Dear Know-It-All, I can't get to school on time"* (Get up earlier?) or *"Dear Know-It-All, my math class is too cold. What should I do?"* (Bring a sweater?) I read the second-to-last one, hoping it wasn't from the last living brain cell in the school:

Dear Know-It-All,

My friend recently asked me for some honest advice and I gave it to her. The problem is that she didn't like the advice, and told me I was wrong, and now is mad at me. I'm okay with her disagreeing with me, but why did she ask me if she didn't really want my opinion? Isn't it okay to have different opinions?

Signed,

Too Honest

Hmm. Is there such a thing as being too honest? I think of the times that Allie was certainly too honest with me, even though sometimes I actually ask for her opinion. It's always annoying to hear something negative. She never misses an opportunity to tell me I need my hair trimmed or cooler shoes, or that I just need to look more like her. But we're sisters, and if we're talking honestly here, I never miss an opportunity to tell her when she looks like she's trying too hard with too much makeup or supertight jeans.

But friends are different. If Hailey asks me if I like her shirt or if she's being too pushy or something, sometimes I tell her the truth and sometimes I don't. It depends on whether I think I'll really upset her or not. She was honest with me this morning and I guess I needed to hear what she told me, so that was okay. Were there really different rules for when to be honest? Or is it that sometimes you shouldn't be *as* honest as other times?

Maybe *I* need to be more truthful. I constantly cover up the Dear Know-It-All column, but that's because I have to. I just manipulated Allie into letting me borrow a shirt. If I turn up the "honesty" volume, will people get upset? Boy, this is a tough one.

I read another letter in a bright red leftover Christmas card envelope:

Dear Know-It-All,

I'm good friends with a boy who I like. We do stuff together, but I never know if it's a date. How do I find out?

Sincerely,

Just Friends?

Yeah, I know a little something about that. Lately, though, I've been wondering if Michael and I even fall into that category anymore, since we haven't spent much time together.

"Sam! Can you help me set the table?" my mom called from the kitchen. I guess the Dear Know-It-All column would have to wait. I stuffed the letters back into my pocket.

The next day, at lunch, Hailey and I sampled the organic sweet potato fries from the premium table, where we can pay extra to get something healthy. Believe it or not, it's usually extra-yummy, too, and I'm talking about things like kale chips, chickpea fritters, and whole-grain carrot muffins. Even Hailey eats it, or some of it, kind of.

"These are awesome," I said, waving a fry in Hailey's face. "Have one."

"Are they mushy?" she asked, leaning back in her chair, arms crossed.

"Just take one!"

"Oh, all right," Hailey said. She sat up and took a bite. Her face lit up. "They're just like regular fries, only, um . . ."

"Sweeter? As in *sweet* potato?"

I looked up and saw Michael come into the cafeteria. He didn't even walk over to our table to say hello, which he usually does, but sat at a table full of guys on the baseball team.

"Is he ignoring me?" I asked.

"No, why would he be?" Hailey said, stealing another one of my fries.

"I don't know. No reason."

"Don't worry. He didn't forget about you when he wrote that story with Austin."

"I know." I just wanted to get back to our routine. For the last issue, Michael worked on a story with Austin Carey about the school district's investments. Now we were skipping this issue. By the time we really got working on it, a month would have gone by since we'd actually spent some quality time together. When you have a crush, it seems like every day something happens to change your situation one way or another.

Hailey must have seen the panic on my face. "Okay, I have an idea. Get out a pen and paper and write down what I say." *Girl Saves Best Friend from Losing Crush!* At least I hoped so. Since Hailey has dyslexia, it's hard for her to write fast. I'm usually the list person.

"'How to Keep Michael Lawrence's Interest,'" she said.

"Shh!" I hissed.

"Okay," she said in a lower tone. "Ask him about the play."

I wrote that down.

"Ask him how baseball is going."

Kind of boring, but maybe.

"Ask him who he has a crush on," she said, as if she were reciting a grocery list to me.

"I don't think so," I said.

"Just write! Show up at his house really hungry and ask if he could make you some cinnamon buns or else you might die of starvation."

"Are you insane?" I rolled my eyes and crumpled up the list.

"Why'd you do that? I was just joking on the

last one," she said. She suddenly seemed kind of hurt. Now I was wondering if my reaction was too honest. I know she was joking on the last one, but *Ask him who he has a crush on*? Really?

"I might do the first two," I said.

"Good!" She perked back up. "Let's get started!"

She grabbed my arm and I stuffed the crumpled paper in my bag. At least I was wearing the cute green shirt and my favorite little silver hoop earrings that I got last year for my birthday.

"What are we doing?" I whispered.

She turned to me and put a finger on her lips. Then she motioned for me to follow her. I did, hoping I wouldn't regret it. We walked over to Michael's table.

"Hi, Michael," Hailey said, and fluffed her hair in her flirty way. Whoa, she'd better not start with that again. At the beginning of the year, she had a crush on Michael, too, but we sorted it out. I gave her a look. Michael turned and saw us.

"Hey, Hailey. Hey, Pasty," he said, and smiled, showing off the dimple in his left cheek.

I just smiled and waved. Then she shoved me toward him and whispered "Baseball!" in my ear.

"So, how's baseball?" I said, trying to look at some of the other boys at the table too so my head wouldn't explode. What did Hailey think she was doing?

Michael looked around, as if he wasn't sure if I was speaking to him or not.

"Um, good?"

"Okay; well then . . . ," I said, my cheeks on fire. "Oh, Hailey, I just remembered something really important that I left in my locker." I grabbed her hand.

"What?" she said, all smiley and oblivious.

"Just something *really* important." I put my arm around her, leading her away from the table.

Michael looked back and forth at each of us. "You okay, Paste?"

"Oh, sure. See ya," I said, and tugged Hailey out of the cafeteria.

"Ow! What's so important?" she said when we finally got out into the hallway.

"Nothing, I just wanted to get out of there. Why

did you do that?" I asked. I put my hands on my warm cheeks. "I felt like such a dork."

"Well, you didn't want him to forget about you," she said. "Hey, I was trying to help. Are you seriously mad?"

I took a deep breath. "No," I lied.

"Are you *sure* you're not mad?"

"I'm sure. Are you coming over this afternoon?" I asked, trying to move off the subject.

"Yup!" she said.

The fifth-period bell rang and we hurried off to our classes before the stampede from the cafeteria took over the hallways, and at this point I hoped I'd never see Michael again. Well, at least not today. It was hard to be honest sometimes, but I didn't want to get into an argument with Hailey. I know she wants the best for me and Michael. Sometimes she can just get a little carried away. Just a bit.

Chapter 3

POSSESSED WASHING MACHINE EATS SECRET LETTERS!

Hailey came over and we did our homework together. Hailey usually needs some help with her homework because of her dyslexia. Afterward she showed me photos of Michael that Jeff, the *Voice* photographer, posted on Buddybook of him goofing around after a baseball game. There was one where he was in his uniform balancing a baseball on his bat, and somehow managing to give the camera a gorgeous smile. I wanted to print it out and make a poster of it. Of course, I had to restrain myself. Imagine if he ever saw I made a poster of him? The probability of him ever seeing my room is probably a big fat zero, but still. Then Hailey had to leave because her mom wanted her home for dinner. Hailey said she wished she could stay because she was probably going home to soy burgers and spinach soufflé, and the smells coming from our kitchen were delicious.

"Potatoes?" Mom asked when Allie and I sat down for dinner. She held out a thick white bowl heaped with her awesome roasted potatoes. She puts these little sprigs of rosemary on them. They rock. She also made steak and sautéed string beans. Mom only makes steak for our birthdays or when we have special guests.

"Mom, what's the occasion?" I asked.

"What do you mean?"

"Steak and everything," I said, taking a small scoop of potatoes.

"No occasion," she said cheerfully. "I just wanted to have a nice dinner with my daughters and catch up. I miss you guys. We've all been so busy."

Mom is a freelance bookkeeper, and sometimes her schedule is pretty light. But sometimes she has to work like crazy, which is how it's been during the past few weeks. We've been grabbing quick dinners at the kitchen counter. When she's really busy, my mom puts something in the fridge for us to heat up in the microwave.

"Allie?" Mom said, holding the bowl in front of her.

"No thanks. I'm going low-carb for the play," Allie said with a toss of her hair, and she heaped up her plate with steak and string beans. Then she nudged her phone out of her jeans pocket and started texting with one hand under the table, her phone on her knee.

"You seriously have a problem," I said.

Mom looked up. "Allie, we're having a media-free dinner."

"But—"

"No buts," Mom said, holding out her hand for Allie's phone. "So, tell us. How's the play going, Miss Low Carb?"

Allie rolled her eyes and gave Mom the phone. Then she took a deep breath and started twirling her long, shiny hair into a bun. Whenever she starts playing with her hair, it's going to be a long story.

"It's okay. I just can't believe I didn't get the part of Maria. I mean, Julia Gowen is okay, but my audition was awesome. She might be able to sing, but she can't dance. She's so awkward. The only reason she got the part was because she and the director's daughter went to some theater camp together last summer and she gets straight A's *and* the director wanted the person who plays the lead to be able to handle it academically. But I could have totally handled it, and I'm a much better dancer." Then she sighed and let her hair spill over her shoulders again.

"But do you like your part?" I asked. Allie was playing the lead's best friend, Anita.

Allie shrugged and took a big bite of the string beans. "It's one of the big roles. But I wish I were Maria."

Allie does a lot of theater, and as much as I hate to admit it, she's a great dancer and a pretty good singer. It's her thing. She always got the lead parts in middle school, and she used to think she was the next Disney starlet before our school district decided to combine both theater programs into one. Now there's a lot more competition for the roles. Allie always gets good parts—sometimes the lead, sometimes a supporting role. Mom says it's more of a challenge to shine in a supporting role, but Allie doesn't agree.

"There's no business like show business!" Mom sang out in a loud, comical voice. I laughed. Allie just rolled her eyes again, but I saw a smile sneaking onto her lips.

After dinner I went into my room to get started on the Dear Know-It-All column. I remembered that I'd stuck the letters into my jeans the day before. I looked on the back of my chair. No jeans. I looked in my closet, where my hamper was. No jeans. My heart started beating fast. Where in the world did I put them?

I headed downstairs to the washer and dryer. *Don't panic, don't panic*, I repeated in my head. Usually, when Mom finished our laundry she put it on the steps for us to take upstairs. I saw a neat little pile of my clothes. I searched through it, but still no jeans. I went down to the laundry room. There was big basket of laundry on the dryer. But even if I found the jeans, wouldn't the letters be destroyed by the washer? *Possessed Washing Machine Eats Secret Letters!* I looked in the basket, and only stacks of sheets stared back at me. The washer was empty and the dryer was empty.

"Mom!" I called as I ran upstairs to the kitchen. She was putting detergent in the dishwasher. She looked up. I glanced around, making sure Allie wasn't there, and told her my problem.

"Hmm. I just saw Allie taking a big pile of laundry upstairs. Maybe I put your jeans in her pile. I can't tell your clothes and Allie's apart these days."

"That means my letters were washed!"

"Oh, sweetheart, I'm sorry. They'll probably still be intact if they were tucked into your pocket. Did you read them already?"

"Yes, but I have to type them exactly the way they were worded."

Off I ran to Allie's room. My mom followed me.

I turned to her. "Mom, if we both go in, she might get suspicious and ask too many questions about why we care so much."

She nodded. "Okay, tell me what happens," she said, and went back to the kitchen.

Right outside Allie's door, which was always closed these days, I took a deep breath. I had to handle this the right way. This was no time for honesty. I knocked on the door.

"What?" Allie yelled.

"Um, can I come in?"

"Why?" she yelled back. "I'm busy!"

"Please?"

I heard her stomp to the door. She flung it open. She wore lots of eyeliner and bright red lipstick, and a robe.

"What on earth are you doing?" I asked, suppressing a smile. My sister can be pretty strange sometimes.

"Actress-related." She went back to her desk and started putting on green eye shadow. "Working on my character."

I looked around for the pile. There it was, on the

corner of her desk! I couldn't tell if my jeans were in there or not. I walked over to her and the pile.

"I think Mom mixed up our clothes in the laundry. Can I just look in this pile?"

"Suit yourself," she said. She was putting a fake beauty mark on the side of her cheek. ***Delusional Sister Believes She's Marilyn Monroe.*** This actress thing was really going to Allie's head. I lifted up a couple of T-shirts and folded sweatpants. Still no jeans. Then, at the very bottom of the pile, I saw them and pulled them out. Score. Now I just had to take them to my room and check the notes.

"Hey!" Allie looked over at me. "Those are mine!" Her arm came at me as fast as a frog's tongue and she snatched the jeans away. My folded-up letters fell out of the pocket, onto the floor. I was relieved that they looked somewhat intact.

We both looked at the floor. I grabbed the Dear Know-It-All letters faster than she swiped the jeans.

"What are those?" Allie wanted to know.

"That proves it. They're my notes and my jeans," I said, clutching the letters tight.

Allie looked more closely at the jeans and the size tag. Even though we're both pretty tall, I wore a smaller size than her.

"Fine," she said. "But what are those notes you're clinging to so passionately? Letters from your boyfriend?" she teased, and tried take them out of my hand.

I held on tight, but was afraid I'd crush them. They felt slightly damp.

"Actually, kind of, yes!" I said.

She stopped trying to grab them. "Really?"

My heart was pulsing in my ears. "Well, from the boy I *wish* was my boyfriend." Just keep talking, Martone. Allie loved to listen to guy gossip.

"Notes professing his undying love for you?" she said, and put her hands over her heart.

"No, just notes for our next assignment."

"I don't know if I believe you. What's the assignment?" she asked, her hands on her hips now, her green-eye-shadowed eyes staring me down.

"Reviewing the, um . . . play?"

Allie took this in for a second. I'm not sure what was going through her mind.

"My play? *West Side Story*?" she finally said.

"That's the one," I said nervously. I just wanted to leave. The letters were getting really sweaty in my hand. "Okay, gotta go!" I announced, and ran out of her room.

"Your jeans!" she called after me. For crying out loud, this was the conversation that would never end. I ran back into her room. She held the jeans up in the air.

"You better give me a good review," she said. "If you don't, you're in big trouble!"

I nodded. I was surprised she would care about what the middle school paper had to say about her and the play.

"Promise?" She held the jeans even higher.

"Yes, yes!" I jumped up and took my jeans.

Finally in the safety of my own room, I examined the letters. They were a bit wrinkled, with the ink a little runny on some of the words, but still readable, thank goodness. Where could

I put them where no one could find them—or wash them, for that matter? After all that drama with Allie, I wouldn't be surprised if she came snooping into my room to find the letters and read them herself. I stuck them under my mattress and collapsed on top of it, too tired to do any work. Older sisters were exhausting. It also seemed like it was getting harder and harder to tell the truth. I hoped I could keep my promise about the play review, or I would have to add another lie to my suddenly growing list of untruths. Lately, it seemed I had the opposite problem that Too Honest did.

Chapter 4

GIRL TELLS THE TRUTH. BEST FRIEND SPONTANEOUSLY COMBUSTS

Hailey came up to me the next day while I was unloading my book bag.

"Hey," she said. Then she leaned against my locker and gave me the once-over. "Why are you looking so blah lately?"

"Gee, thanks. Good morning to you, too."

"I just think you need to be more proactive," she said.

Oh no, this meant she had an idea. Whenever she used big words, that meant she was going to try to convince me of something. Sometimes I get a little tired from Hailey's energy. That's part of the reason she's so good at sports. She needs to put all that energy somewhere. I've never been a morning person. It usually takes me until third period to feel fully awake. I checked her out. Her hair was still a little wet from the shower, and she was looking bright-eyed as she always did, but maybe too bright-eyed.

I took out my earthonomics folder and put it in my bag. Then I stood up. "What are you talking about? How proactive am I supposed to be at eight in the morning? And about what?"

She started putting her stuff in her locker. "Well, just look at you."

Now she sounded like Allie. I only needed one person in my life giving me unsolicited fashion advice, and usually it was the other way around. Hailey was always asking me for advice on her outfits. I looked down at myself. I was wearing respectable dark jeans, a long gray cardigan, and black flats. Maybe not bright and peppy, but I'm the writer. Aren't writers supposed to be kind of dark?

"At least I'm wearing lip gloss. What about you, Miss Fashion Plate?" I said, eyeing her plain white T-shirt, jeans, and Converse sneakers.

"Look." She leaned in close and lowered her voice. "I don't care what you wear. But I remember how sad you got when Michael wrote a story with Austin and you had no time with him. You need to make yourself more noticeable. You look like . . . like a rainy day."

I sighed a big sigh. Apparently Hailey did not have a problem with saying whatever she thought. Maybe she should answer the Dear Know-It-All letters. I looked down at my dark, dull clothes. Maybe she was right. Maybe she had more of a knack for fashion than I gave her credit for. *Sporty Soccer Player Becomes Famous Stylist.*

"And there he is," she said, jumping up and down. "Pinch your cheeks. I read somewhere that it brightens up your face."

I finished packing up and putting away what I needed. I stood up again. I was not pinching my cheeks. People in old-fashioned English novels pinch their cheeks. Samantha Martone does not.

Michael was walking with Jamal Williams, one of his friends from the baseball team. He waved to us and walked over. I was about to say a nice, normal "Hi" when Hailey shoved me in the back, pushing me toward Michael. Now, Hailey may have meant this to be a gentle shove—a shove that says to the person getting shoved "Go for it" or "You can do it"—but sometimes Hailey doesn't know her own strength.

"Oof!" I couldn't help but yell out, and suddenly I was standing about a centimeter away from Michael Lawrence. I did manage to get a whiff of the shampoo he must have used and the scent of Tide, which has become one of the best smells in the world for me. I hope I smelled just as good. I certainly didn't mind being so close to Michael, but I wanted to be close on my own terms. I stepped back and smoothed my hair, hoping my cheeks weren't as red as cherries. What was Hailey thinking?

"Easy there, Trippy," Michael said, smiling, because I guess he's just used to me being clumsy.

"You okay?" Jamal asked in a worried way, genuinely concerned.

"Uh, yeah. I'm fine. Guess I tripped on something,"

I said through gritted teeth, giving Hailey a sideways look.

"She's fine and I'm fine. We're all fine!" Hailey said in an extra-cheery way. "Sam, what was that thing about the play that you wanted to ask Michael?"

My mind immediately raced. What exactly was she talking about? I opened my mouth, but I really didn't know what to say.

"You know, that thing . . . about . . . the . . . play?" she said really slowly.

"Right, yeah!" I finally said. "The play. I guess we both need to see the play."

"Can we talk about it at lunch? Jamal and I have a huge test in language arts first thing. We wanted to go over a couple of notes before class."

"It's a date!" Hailey called out.

Michael looked at her, and then back at me.

"Okay, um . . . well, see you both then," he said as he and Jamal walked away. My head was spinning. I watched Michael and Jamal until they rounded a corner.

"Who are you, and what have you done with my

friend Hailey?" I said as we both started walking toward our classes.

"What do you mean?"

I stopped walking and faced her. "Well, it's just that you shoved me toward him and I was planning to bring up the play soon anyway. Now he thinks we're both meeting him at lunch to talk about the play, which is weird."

"Look, you were so bummed out when he wrote that story with Austin. I'm just trying to help things get back on track with you two. Do you want the same thing to happen all over again? The early bird gets the worm." She obviously cared a lot about me and Michael, but I just wasn't sure about her approach.

"So I'm the bird and Michael's the worm?"

"Exactly," she said, looking pleased with herself and not getting my sarcasm at all.

I started walking again. "I don't know, Hailey."

"Just trust me. He won't be able *not* to think about you."

"I just think we're being a little too proactive." I took a deep breath. Here goes nothing. "Sometimes you get a little charged up about things. I just want to handle this my own way."

"I do not get too charged up about things! Are you just going to stand there and let life pass you by?! I've been watching you two dance around each other forever."

We came to our classrooms, mine next to us and hers across the hall. "I guess you're right," I said, looking down.

"Attagirl!" she said, and slapped me on the back.

"Ow."

"Sorry," she said. We walked into our classrooms. I just didn't have the heart to go any further with the issue. *Girl Tells the Truth. Best Friend Spontaneously Combusts.* At least that's what it felt like would happen. I didn't realize I was this wimpy. And I didn't realize Hailey was so bad at taking what she dishes out.

At lunchtime I walked into the cafeteria and looked around. I was hoping to see Michael before

I saw Hailey so she wouldn't get all "proactive" on me. He was sitting at a table with Jamal and a couple of other guys from the baseball team. Maybe he forgot about our Hailey-arranged lunch date. I looked around for another place to sit and heard my name, or my rather lovely nickname, from behind me.

"Hey, Pasty, I was just hanging with them until I saw you. Want to sit here and talk about the play?"

My shoulders, which must have been next to my ears, relaxed. Finally I had Michael all to myself in what felt like a really long time.

"Yes!" I said, a little too enthusiastically.

"Should we wait for Hailey?" he asked. That's just one more thing I like about Michael. He's always a nice guy.

"No, she'll be here soon," I said, kind of hoping she'd skip lunch for some unknown reason. I felt guilty as soon as I had the thought.

We put our bags down at the table and stood on line. We both decided to get the organic option— rice-and-bean burritos with fresh salsa. Yum.

After we brought our trays back to our table, I saw Hailey walk in. I hoped she wouldn't come and do something like shove my chair even closer to Michael's than it already was. She seemed like she was walking toward us, and then she suddenly sat down with a few girls we were friends with. I caught her eye and motioned her over, but she just gave me a thumbs-up and started chatting it up with our friends. That's Hailey for you. Just when she does something to drive me crazy, she makes up for it big-time.

"So, the play is in two weeks," I said. "When should we see it?" I hoped he wouldn't think this was too forward of me, or that I was asking him to see it with me.

"Well, when were you planning to see it?"

I hadn't really thought about the logistics of this. Okay, if I'm being *honest*, I did think of the logistics and thought that Michael and I should go to see the play together, like an almost date, even if it might be a working one. I even thought of the perfect outfit to wear, a flowing white peasant blouse, black leggings, and Allie's black suede boots if she'd let me. The way Michael asked his question, it did not seem like he had the same plan in mind.

"Oh, well, since my sister's in it, probably opening night?" I said, wondering if I should have just said I didn't know.

"Great! That's just what I was thinking," he said, and took a big bite of his burrito. He couldn't talk, because he was chewing, so I took a bite of mine and sweated out the next few seconds while I wondered what he was thinking. I finished my bite first.

"So we'll both go that night?" I ventured. Hailey would be proud of me for being so proactive.

He laughed, "No, no. I thought you meant that you would go then, and I could go for the second performance. It would make a much fairer review. That's what a lot of professional reviewers do— they go a few times to get a well-rounded picture. We wouldn't want to give them a bad review if opening night didn't go so well but the other two performances did."

As much as it made my heart hurt, the journalist

in me knew he was right. We had to see more than one performance, and it probably didn't make sense for the two of us to go to both. I nodded back at him, not able to summon the energy to actually say yes.

"So you go opening night and I'll go to the Saturday matinee. I believe we have a plan," he said with a pleased look on his face, taking another bite of burrito as if he didn't have a care in the world. He grinned and held out his free hand for a high five.

"Awesome. Sounds perfect," I said, trying to muster up a smile and gave his hand a slap. I saw Hailey out of the corner of my eye and she gave me another thumbs-up, probably thinking I was having a blast. I examined my half-eaten burrito, but I wasn't really hungry anymore. Hailey was going to love hearing the real story. *Young Reporter Attempts to Win "Proactive" Medal. Fails Miserably.*

Chapter 5

INNOCENT GIRL DISCOVERS SHE'S A BIG FAT LIAR

I didn't talk to Hailey for the rest of the day. I knew she was dying to know how my conversation with Michael went, but I just needed time to think about it. She left the cafeteria before me anyway, and then had soccer practice right after school. I was sitting in my bedroom, turning it over and over in my head. What could I have done differently? Should I just have come out and said to Michael, "Why don't we go together on opening night?" But the truth is, I didn't want to have to be so . . . well, honest.

An IM from Hailey popped up on the screen. **Are you avoiding me???**

Of course not! I sort of lied. I wanted to spend more time with Hailey, and normally I couldn't get enough boy talk, but lately I'd been wishing she'd back off from the Michael thing a little.

So are you and Michael going to the play?

Sigh. I spun around in my desk chair a few times before giving my superexciting answer. Not.

Yeah, on separate nights, I answered.

What??? So bummed for u!

It's ok. Better for the review, I wrote back. But it wasn't okay. For some reason, I didn't feel like telling that to Hailey just yet.

After dinner Allie walked around the house "in character," dressed up as Anita from *West Side Story*, wig, fake eyelashes, and all, rehearsing her lines and songs. She said it helped her get into character to walk around the house as if she were Anita. I decided it would be a good time to hang out in my room. I noticed my mom was hidden away in her office as well. I decided to get started on the Dear Know-It-All letter. Here went nothing. I gently opened the fragile, freshly washed notebook paper it was written on and read it again.

Dear Too Honest, I typed.

There isn't anything wrong with being honest with your friend.

Then I just stared at my computer screen. I had no idea what to say, and we needed to run something for next week.

The following day we had a meeting in the *Voice* office with Mr. Trigg. Trigger wanted to see how his crazy idea was going. I didn't want to sit next to Michael. It just made me sad to think that my one chance of going to a play with Michael Lawrence was already dead in the water. I got there first, as usual, and just as I was sitting down, there he was.

"Hey there, P," he said, slightly out of breath, and he plopped himself right down next to me. His hair fell into his eyes and he tossed his head in a particularly adorable way. This only made me feel more sorry for myself.

"How's the switcheroo going, lads? Easy peasy?" Mr. Trigg asked. Everyone grew quiet. Nobody, in fact, said anything.

"Hello out there?" he said. "Does that mean everything is hunky-dory?"

"Well, it's definitely harder than I thought," said one of the sports reporters now covering news.

"Yeah!" said an arts reporter covering sports. "I never knew it was so complicated to cover a sports game."

"I knew this was going to be a disaster," I whispered in Michael's ear. He just smiled; then Mr. Trigg looked at me. I hoped he hadn't heard what I said.

"Ah, see? I'm keeping you on your toes," he said to the group. "The worst thing for any journalist is to be too familiar with a subject beforehand. That stops you from asking interesting questions, thinking about things from all angles. Change is good. It helps you get closer to the truth."

I hope so, I thought. Afterward, Mr. Trigg had us break up into groups and discuss any problems we were having with our stories. I couldn't discuss the problem I was having with my Dear Know-It-All letter and Michael and I hadn't started our piece yet, so we just listened to some of the issues other people were having. Some of the arts writers complained that in a news story they couldn't voice their opinions. *Duh*, I thought. Some of the newswriters complained that writing a sports story didn't allow for any research, which some of the sportswriters said was wrong. All in all, it seemed that no one was really happy. I wanted to wait until everyone was gone so I could talk to Mr. Trigg and check and see if there were any new Dear Know-It-All letters.

After our meeting was done, Michael turned to me. "You walking out?"

"Not yet. I have to ask Mr. Trigg something."

Michael stared at me for a moment. I've always wondered if he's known all along that I'm Dear Know-It-All, but he's never come out and asked me.

"Oh, okay. I'll catch you later, Paste," he said, and bounded out the door.

Yeah, later, like in after the play that we're not going to together.

"So what can I do you for?" Mr. Trigg said after everyone had left. "How's the column treating you?" He took a sip of tea out of his mug, which had a British flag on it, and leaned back in his chair.

I sat down in a chair near his desk and took a deep breath. Suddenly I felt tired. It had been an exhausting week, but I wasn't even sure why.

"That good, huh?" he said, and winked at me while taking another sip of tea. "Tea?" he offered.

"No thanks. I'm okay, but I have a tough letter that I want to answer this week. I didn't think it was so tough, but the more I think about it, the more I'm not sure how to answer it."

"So why don't you answer another letter?" he asked. This was weird. Mr. Trigg was all about going after the hard stuff.

I considered this for a moment. "I think I just need more time," I said, getting up and going over to my secret box. I looked toward the door to make sure no one was coming in to catch me red-handed. Then I opened it and two new letters were sitting there patiently, waiting for me to take them out.

"What's the difficult one about?" Mr. Trigg said.

"Honesty. A girl's friend asked her for her opinion and she gave it, but then the friend told her she was wrong. She wondered why the friend asked for her advice in the first place," I said, sitting down again and stuffing the new letters in my bag.

"Ah, the old 'Tell me what you really think' trick," he said, leaning back in his chair and putting his hands behind his head. "So what's hard for you about answering it?"

"I realized that I have a hard time getting through the day being truly honest. I feel like I'm always hiding the truth to protect others' feelings. Do people really want to hear the truth?"

"Do you?" Mr. Trigg asked.

I bit my lip and thought for a second.

"Yes," I said. "I think I do."

"Well, maybe that's why you're a good writer.

You're not afraid of hearing the truth. You might be afraid of telling it, though."

After I left Mr. Trigg's office, I couldn't stop thinking about the conversation I had with him. If I wasn't afraid of hearing the truth, why was it so hard to tell it sometimes?

I stopped by Hailey's practice, and she was just finishing up. I waved. She waved back.

"Want to walk home together?" I called. She nodded and ran off to get her things.

She joined me and we walked for a minute in silence. I could hear the wind blowing through the trees. The spring air smelled sweet and fresh, and put me in a better mood. "Do you always tell the truth?" I asked her after a while. She was fishing something out of her bag. She stopped and looked up, a pack of gum in her hand.

"Sure, I guess. Well, maybe not *always*."

She held the pack out toward me. I took a piece, unwrapped it, and put it in my mouth. It was one of those weird flavors that Hailey always buys, like kiwi-melon or something like that. I preferred straight-up mint, but chewed it anyway.

"What about you? And why in the world are you asking me this?" she said, chomping on her gum. She looked at me questioningly.

"I don't know. You just seem to say whatever's on your mind so easily."

"I do?" Hailey stopped walking and looked at me. "That's what I think about you."

My mouth hung open for a second. "Really? I feel like I think something, but then change it before it comes out of my mouth. Especially with Michael."

"But we all do that with boys. I hope you don't do that with me!" she said, and looked at me hard.

"No, of course not," I said, and crossed my fingers behind my back. *Innocent Girl Discovers She's a Big Fat Liar.*

"Phew! Because what's the point of having a best friend if you don't tell each other what you really think? Want to come over? We could make a new list of ways to get Michael's attention. I have some more ideas."

"Sure," I said. What was going on with me these days that I couldn't even tell my bestie how I really felt?

Hailey's list was kind of the same as it was the first time. She did have one possible idea, though. She offered to fake being sick on the opening night of the play so I could call Michael at the last minute and ask to go with him. The only problem was that I could easily just go with another friend or my mother on opening night. He wouldn't buy it. Hailey promised she would come up with a better plan. After that, I tried to change the subject to who she liked these days, but no one was catching her eye at the moment. Then I had to go home and finish boatloads of homework.

That night I tried going to sleep early, but Allie was practicing one of her *West Side Story* songs in her room and I couldn't sleep. I went into my mom's room. She was organizing her closets and had piles of sweaters and shirts and pants and skirts everywhere on her bed. I found a small square of a spot near her pillows and sat down cross-legged.

"What's up, honey? You look tired. You okay?"

"Just thinking about stuff," I said, and watched my mom fold an old red sweater of hers and put it in what she said was the "donate" pile.

"Mom, why does Allie get so obsessed with her part when she's in a play? I can't sleep, listening to her sing the same song over and over."

"Oh, you know how she gets before a show. She's nervous."

"She doesn't act nervous. She acts like a diva actress who's won three Academy Awards."

"Well, that's how Allie shows her nerves."

I wondered what I did when I was nervous. Usually I didn't want to be around people or attract any attention. Allie seemed just the opposite.

"Want to talk about whatever you're thinking about?"

"No," I said. "I think I just need some sleep. Can you tell Miss Diva to quiet down? If I tell her, she'll get mad and just sing louder."

"Okay." Mom smiled. "Good night." She came over to kiss me on my forehead. "You'll figure it out. You always do. But let me know if you want to talk about it, okay, honey?"

I nodded and got up.

I climbed into bed and thought of all the things I was trying to figure out with Hailey, with the letter to Dear Know-It-All, with Michael, even with Allie. My eyelids felt heavy and I started to drift off.

Hopefully, it would all seem simpler in the morning.

Chapter 6

GIRL CHOKES ON PEANUT BUTTER, MISSES GREAT DATE OPPORTUNITY

The next morning I wore my favorite long brown skirt and white T-shirt. I had a big breakfast of eggs, toast, and turkey sausage. The weather was sunny and beautiful, and I wasn't going to let anything bother me today.

"Heeellooo!" I said brightly to Hailey when I saw her walking down the hall to her language arts class.

"Hi!" she answered back, and we walked together. Then Hailey pulled me toward the wall. "Okay, I just saw Michael coming the other way. I have another plan about the show. I'll fake sick and say your mom's back is out. She's had back problems before, right? So I'll say you're not sure what to do and he'll offer to go with you on Friday. Is that proactive or what?"

"Well, I don't know about—" I started to say, but again I got one of those Hailey shoves that could have sent me airborne. I found myself colliding with Michael as he came innocently walking down the hall, his head buried in a notebook he was holding.

"Whoa," he said, and steadied me with a hand on my shoulder. His hand felt warm and strong, but I was getting angry—okay, *furious*—at this pushing strategy Hailey actually seemed to think was a proactive plan of attack.

"You okay, Trippy? You've been extra-trippy lately, even for you," he said. Then that cute, crazy smile emerged, along with crinkles near his eyes—the whole deal.

I backed up, stood up straight, and cleared my throat.

"I—well, it's just that . . ." I looked behind me, planning on glaring at Hailey, but she was nowhere to be seen.

"I'm glad I ran into you—not literally, but I guess kind of literally," he said.

"Ha-ha."

"Well, I'm glad, because I was thinking about the play."

I stopped breathing. Maybe Hailey had been right all along—all this pushing and awkward conversation had kept me on his mind. There's no such thing as bad publicity, right?

"Yeah?" I said, toeing the carpet with the tip of my ballet flat, trying to stay cool. No biggie.

"We should both probably see it twice," he said, and started stuffing his notebook into his backpack. The bell for class rang.

"Okay, why?" I asked, my mind quickly trying to decipher what he actually meant.

"Because . . . ," he started to say. "You know what? Let's talk later. I don't want to be late for class."

I nodded and we both rushed off. Great— now I had to spend the entire earthonomics class wondering what exactly he was talking about.

At lunchtime I went tearing around to find

Hailey and practically ran her over on the way to the cafeteria.

"So he wants to go twice," I said breathlessly when I saw her. She was walking with our friend Jenna.

"See? I knew it was working!" Hailey exclaimed.

"What's working? I'm not even sure what he means," I said.

"Well, how many shows are there?" she asked.

Jenna answered for me. "Three!" I kind of wished Jenna wasn't there. She knew I had a massive crush on Michael, but usually I kept the details between me and Hailey. I looked at her, and then at Hailey again.

"Right—opening night on Friday, Saturday matinee, and Saturday night. So if you both go to two shows," Hailey said, now sounding like an elementary school math teacher, "you have to overlap once!"

"I guess so," I said, not knowing why this hadn't occurred to me.

"So that's great!" Hailey said, shaking my arm.

"No, it isn't," I said.

"What is it?" she asked. "What's wrong?"

I wanted to just come out and say that even though this development was fantastic, she had to stop being so pushy, both literally and figuratively. But I couldn't really get into that with Jenna there, hanging on every word.

"Nothing," I said.

"So this is what I think you should do," she said, leaning toward me. Jenna leaned in too. "Next time you see him," Hailey continued in a low, conspiratorial tone, "bring it up, the whole thing about going to two shows, but don't ask him if he wants to go to the Friday night one together. Just say, 'Well, I'm going Friday night and you're going Saturday afternoon . . .' and then let him fill in the rest. He'll just have to ask you to the Saturday night performance."

"Perfect plan!" said Jenna..

I had to admit it was a perfect plan. "Thanks, Hails," I said, and meant it.

Michael was nowhere to be seen in the cafeteria. I wondered where he could be. Sometimes he crammed for a test in the hallway with a friend.

Sometimes he had a team meeting. He could be anywhere. I hoped I'd see him soon. Tickets were selling out fast.

Two days went by and I still hadn't had a face-to-face conversation with Michael Lawrence. Then I was home, spreading peanut butter on a banana for a snack in the kitchen, when the phone rang. My hands were all peanut-buttery and I couldn't answer. A few seconds later, Allie came sauntering into the kitchen. She didn't walk anymore, she *sauntered.* She covered the receiver and came over to me.

"It's your boyfriend," she whispered in my ear. I glared at her and grabbed the phone.

"Hello," I said. Unfortunately, I had just taken a bite of peanut butter and banana and my voice sort of sounded like it was underwater. ***Girl Chokes on Peanut Butter, Misses Great Date Opportunity.***

"Sam?" he said. Michael never called me Sam. "Is that you?"

"Yeah, hold on," I said. I put the phone down

and gulped a glass of water. Then I got on the phone again, sounding like myself. "Hi, sorry."

"Peanut butter?" he asked.

"How did you know?" I said, surprised.

"Oh, I know. I'm a huge fan of after-school peanut butter snacks."

I laughed, and he laughed too. It was so nice to joke around with Michael. It had been a long time since we'd just chilled out together rather than awkwardly colliding in the hallways.

"So, as I was saying the other day, we really should see every show and each see it twice. The fuller the coverage, the better. Your sister's in it, right? What part does she have?"

"I agree. We should definitely each see it twice," I said, just so there could be no change of plan. Thank goodness there weren't four shows. "Allie's Anita, Maria's best friend."

"I've never seen *West Side Story*, but I assume it's a good part. I saw Allie in *Bye Bye Birdie* last year. She was great."

Wow, I couldn't believe he remembered that! I can barely keep track of what Allie's been in.

"Yeah, she was. Okay, so there's a performance Friday night, Saturday afternoon, and Saturday night. I'd planned to go on Friday night, and you're going on Saturday afternoon," I said, and then was silent. Operation Hailey's Plan.

"Right," he said. Then nothing. Then more nothing. This was the part he was supposed to fill in! I debated on whether to shove the whole banana into my mouth so I wouldn't have to talk. I had to fill the void. A silent second on the telephone is equal to an hour of regular time, in my book.

"Um, so we should probably go together on Saturday night?" My voice became really high and squeaky on "night." Oh no, did I just ask him out? I should really keep my mouth filled with peanut butter at all times.

"Sounds good!" he said, all chipper. "I'll meet you there."

After we hung up, I sat in silence and ate the rest of my banana. Hailey was not going to be happy.

I waited until that night to tell her.

Why didn't u follow the plan?? she wailed

through the computer after I'd IM'd her the whole story.

I did!

But is it a date or not? she asked.

It's just a work/school thing anyway. Wasn't supposed to be a date, I argued. I had to defend myself.

We'll c. New plan tomrw.

I sighed. I hoped her plan didn't include shoving me across the hallway or asking Michael ridiculous questions.

I hopped onto my bed and closed the door. I had to get the Dear Know-It-All letter in by Friday. I could save Too Honest for the next issue. I read a couple of new letters I just got, but they were not going to fly: *"I never like the organic option in the cafeteria"* (Don't eat it?). *"I hate blue nail polish and it's the only kind I have at home."* (Buy a new bottle?) I had to answer the question I was all too familiar with, and lately so familiar with that I was afraid Hailey would think I had written it. Better than thinking I was Dear Know-It-All. I spun around in my chair a couple of times and stared at the black screen. Then I took a deep breath and went for it. I wrote the answer quickly, all in one pass. Sometimes it's better not to think too much.

Dear Just Friends?,

When you spend a lot of time with someone that you might want to date, it's hard to know what's what. I guess if he asks you out, or if you ask him out somewhere, it's considered a date. If you both decide together, like friends would, then it's not. Maybe don't suggest anything to do for a while. Let him fill in the blanks and see what happens. Good luck!

I don't know if my answer was groundbreaking, but it made sense to me, even if it didn't actually work for me. At least I had something for the column this week.

Chapter 7

SOCCER PLAYER ASKS OUT BEST FRIEND'S CRUSH BY ACCIDENT!

★ ★ ★

"Brilliant," Hailey said when the issue of the *Voice* came out. She was sitting on a barstool in my kitchen and we were sharing a bowl of popcorn. "Just brilliant!" she said again, and nudged me in the arm.

Friend Possessed by British School Newspaper Advisor. "You sound like Mr. Trigg. What are you talking about?" I asked.

"You sneaky girl."

"What?" I said again, and looked over her shoulder. She was reading the Dear Know-It-All letter.

"You wrote this, didn't you?"

Uh-oh, here we go, but I had been through this

before. *Just stay calm, Martone. Luckily no one suspects you are Dear Know-It-All.* At least I didn't think that's what Hailey meant.

"What do you mean?" I asked innocently.

"You wrote in just to get Mr. Lawrence's attention. He'll see this and maybe get the idea to ask you formally to the play this Saturday! Why didn't I think of that?"

I stopped holding my breath. At least she didn't think I was Dear Know-It-All. The truth was much harder to hide.

"What makes you think I wrote the letter?" I said, purposely being a little coy. Might as well have a little fun.

"See! I knew it! Why didn't you tell me?"

"Listen, Hailey. I didn't write this letter to Dear Know-It-All, and there's no way Michael will read this and ask me to the play on Saturday night when we've already decided to go!" Then I took a huge handful of popcorn and shoved it into my mouth. I actually prayed Michael wouldn't think I wrote this letter.

"All right, all right. Don't freak out," she said,

her eyes gleaming. "I just might have a new plan. Tomorrow, in the morning, hang out by his locker, and wear that cute white peasant blouse, and ask him who he's going to see—"

I cut her off. I just couldn't take another plan.

"Hailey, can I be really honest?" I said, taking a deep breath.

"Yeah?" she said, looking surprised.

At that moment, Allie came bounding into the kitchen in full costume. The swingy purple dress, a dark-haired wig, fake eyelashes, and everything.

"You look amazing!" Hailey squealed. She did, but I was over it.

"Thanks!" she said, and started singing her big number, "America," at the top of her lungs. She started her dance routine, leaped across the kitchen, twirled, grabbed Hailey, and started taking turns dancing with us, spinning us around. We all began to crack up. Then Allie screamed. Hailey and I froze.

"What?" I cried.

"There's a stain on my dress!" Allie said, looking down at the shiny purple material. I saw a tiny little grayish smear, no bigger than a dime, on the skirt part just below her waist. "It's a grease stain. What did you freaks get on me?" she said to us, her eyes practically spinning in her head, her cheeks red and flushed.

"Nothing!" Hailey said, and held her hands up like she was being arrested.

"And you?" Allie turned to me.

"Allie, calm down, you can barely see it. We didn't even touch your dress!"

"Humph," Allie said with a toss of her head. Then she straightened up her wig. "I'm going to be late for dress rehearsal. What am I going to do?" she said holding up the section of skirt. She walked over to the sink and dabbed it with a sponge.

"Allie, seriously. You can't even see it. You're losing a little perspective here," I said. I was getting sick of Miss Diva, her wig, her fake eyelashes, her singing at the top of her lungs every night, *and* her mood swings.

"Don't tell me I'm losing perspective. You're losing perspective! The play is this Friday. It's Tuesday, and now I've got a stain on my costume."

With that she tossed the sponge in the sink and hurried out of the kitchen. We both stared at each other, speechless, and jumped a bit when the front door slammed as Allie exited the house.

"Whoa. Who kidnapped your sister and replaced her with that crazy girl?" Hailey asked.

"It's been like this for weeks. One minute she's all excited, and singing and prancing around the house. The next minute she's yelling at everyone. My mom says it's just nerves, but I kind of can't wait until the play is over."

"I don't blame you. Was she like this for the last show?"

"I think it gets worse every time," I said.

Hailey looked at me carefully. "So what did you want to tell me before that tornado named Allie blew through here?"

I swallowed. Suddenly it just wasn't the right time to tell her how I had been feeling about all her Michael "help."

"Oh, I forget. No biggie," I said, and stuffed another handful of popcorn into my mouth so I wouldn't say another word.

The next day Hailey and I were having lunch in the cafeteria when we both saw Michael coming in. He looked around, saw us, and waved. Then he stopped at the food line. I hoped he'd come and sit with us. I started sending him "come and sit with me" vibes as I watched him load up his tray. But then I wondered if he'd say anything about the letter. My throat started to feel thick and uncomfortable. I swallowed.

"So I have an idea. For when Michael gets here," Hailey said excitedly, breaking my concentration.

"All we ever talk about is me and Michael," I said. "What about your love life these days?"

"After all that ridiculousness with Danny, I'm lying low for a while."

Last month Hailey fell for this new guy, Danny Burke. He seemed really into her and they even went to the movies, but then we found out he was acting like that with about a thousand other girls. It turned out he was just lonely, moving to a new town and everything, and was just trying to make friends. The problem was, the girls didn't know that. He learned his lesson and toned his Romeo act down, but it was a bummer for Hailey. Her crushes never seem to end well.

"So let me tell you before he comes over," she said in a hushed tone, leaning in. "Ask him who he's going with on Saturday afternoon. Good conversation starter."

Before I could answer, he was there with his tray.

"Well, if it isn't double trouble," he said. "Can I sit here?"

"Of course," Hailey said.

Michael sat down, a chair's length away from me and Hailey. He picked up his slice of the spinach-and-cheese whole-grain pizza from the organic option table.

"It's really good," I said, pointing to the pizza.

"Mmm-hmm," he said, his mouth full of pizza.

Then suddenly I felt my chair slide left. In a second, I wasn't a chair's length away anymore, but about an inch away from Michael's. I turned and saw Hailey's foot on my chair.

"Sorry," she said. "I was resting my foot there. I guess I don't know my own strength."

"Guess not," I said, all tense. I inched my chair back.

"So, Michael," she said. "Excited about the big show this weekend?"

"Sure," he said. "Aren't you guys? Allie must be too. How's rehearsal going?"

I had just taken a bite of pizza. I chewed a bit more. I felt like I was choking down my food while I was trying to talk to Michael. I gestured with my hand as if I was going to talk, but I was afraid that if I started too early, Michael was going to get a view of my chewed-up pizza and spinach in my teeth. Gorgeous.

"What I think Sam is trying to say is, who are you going with on Saturday afternoon?" Hailey crossed her legs and pulled her buttered bagel closer to her. Hailey pretty much existed on bread and rice in the cafeteria.

"Why? Do you need a date?" he said to her, a smile spreading across his face.

Wow, this was just getting worse. *Soccer Player Asks Out Best Friend's Crush by Accident!*

"No!" she said. "I'm going with Sam on Friday. But I know you guys are seeing two shows for the review."

"Wait—seriously, why are you asking? Pasty, can you still make it on Saturday night?" Michael asked, looking at me with a genuinely worried expression.

"Yeah, of course," I said, feeling somewhat more relaxed.

"And we're not asking for any particular reason," Hailey added. "We're just making conversation."

"Oh. Well, in that case, I'm going with a couple of guys on the baseball team," he said, and took another bite of pizza.

"Cool," I said. Wow, some conversation we were having. My mind raced for something else to say.

"Sorry to eat and run, but I have to meet Jamal. He wants to see my language arts notes."

"Okay," I said.

"See you Saturday night, Paste. Don't be late," he said, flashing another adorable smile as he stood and picked up his tray.

I got a fluttering feeling in my stomach. Even if he hadn't asked me on a real date, we were still going out together on Saturday night, just me and Michael. Who knows what would happen?

"I won't," I said, trying to give him a sparkly smile back, praying I didn't have spinach stuck in my teeth.

"She won't!" Hailey called while he was walking away.

I couldn't keep my mouth shut anymore.

"Hailey, remember how I said I had something to tell you yesterday? And then Allie came in and went psycho on us?"

"Sure," she said, smiling, her legs pulled up on her chair.

I took a deep breath. I seemed to be taking a lot of those lately.

"Well, I didn't forget what I wanted to say. I was just a little afraid. But I have to be honest."

Hailey put her legs down, and her face got serious.

"What's up?"

"You need to dial down the Michael plans and pushing me closer to him and all that. It's driving me crazy!"

Her face went red. She looked as though I had punched her.

"I thought you wanted my help," she said, her voice shaky.

"I did. I do! I love scheming about boy stuff with you. But it's just gotten to be a bit much lately. I can handle Michael myself sometimes."

"Well, you're always complaining how you never get to spend enough time with him. Maybe I'm tired of listening to that all the time. Maybe that's gotten to be a little too much for me. If you guys would just go on a stupid date, I wouldn't have to listen to you complain all the time." She crossed her arms and pressed her mouth shut.

"You said I should be honest!" I was starting to feel awful.

"Fine, see how you do on your own," she said, getting up. She took her stuff and started to leave.

"Hailey, come on," I called, standing up.

She turned around and held her hand up. "I think we need a little space. How's that for honesty?" she said. I stopped in my tracks and watched her walk out the cafeteria doors. That went well.

That night in bed, I was still trying to piece together what happened. We didn't see each other after the scene in the cafeteria. She had practice after school, and I went straight home. All afternoon, while I did my homework, I kept sneaking glances at the computer, hoping she'd IM me, but no such luck. I didn't IM her, either.

I wrapped my down comforter around me tight. I could hear Allie's faint singing over the fan I had switched on to drown out her voice. So much for saying what I really was thinking, but maybe Hailey was right. Maybe we did need a little space from each other.

Chapter 8

SCHOOL PLAY OPENS, EVERYONE SURVIVES

It was finally Friday, the day of the first performance of the play. Hailey and I hadn't really talked since our big argument. We'd managed to avoid each other yesterday. I didn't even go into the cafeteria at lunchtime. Instead I hid out in the *Voice* office, making a checklist of what I was going to look for in evaluating the play:

Overall singing quality
Choreography
Set design
Costumes
Lighting
Lead actress's performance
Lead actor's performance
Main supporting role
    performances

I tapped my pen, trying to think of anything I could be forgetting. Mr. Trigg walked in.

"Why, hello there, Ms. Martone," he said. "How are we on the day of the big show?"

"I'm okay," I said. "Just making a list of things I want to look for when I see it." I looked at my list again, and wrote down *Sound engineering?*

"I did a few theater reviews back in the day," he said, sitting down and unwinding the striped scarf he always wore around school, but for some reason never in the *Voice* office. "Nothing beats going to see a show in the West End in London. I highly recommend it if you ever get the chance."

"Can I ask you a question, Mr. Trigg?" I said while I put my notes away.

"Fire away," he said.

"What if the play's not good and we have to write about that? I don't want to hurt people's feelings," I said.

"Just tell it like you see it," he said, "and you'll be brilliant."

I nodded and thanked him, but I wasn't so sure about my brilliance.

At home my mom and I ate a quick dinner that was actually kind of a breakfast—scrambled eggs, toast, and salad. Allie had gone over to the high school auditorium that afternoon to get ready, so we hadn't seen her since the morning. I was kind of glad she hadn't come home. She probably would have been bouncing off the walls, as my mom says. In about half an hour, we were going to pick Hailey up and drive her to the show. I was nervous. I wasn't sure what we were going to say to each other. I had to tell my mom what was going on. I put my fork down.

"Hailey and I kind of got into a little argument," I said, picking up my fork again and poking at my eggs.

Mom held her fork frozen in the air between her mouth and her plate. "Uh-oh, how little?" she said, looking worried.

"Well, not so little," I said, and stabbed a cucumber from my salad.

"Okay, how big?"

"Hailey was bugging me about something, so I told her it was bothering me. She got really upset and told me I was bugging her too, and then we decided that we needed some space, and now we haven't talked in two days. She said I could be honest with her, and she always tells me what she thinks—a little too much sometimes. So why did she get so upset?" I said it all in one breath, then leaned back in my chair. It felt good to get it out.

"Hmm. Are you still upset with her?" Mom asked, taking our plates to the garbage pail and scraping the food off. Then she started putting them in the dishwasher.

"I don't know, not really. I just want to work it out. She was pretty mad. But she said I should tell her the truth. That's what best friends are for, right?"

"Well, sometimes. The truth is always good, but we have to decide what we can let go and what we can't. Was she mad or hurt? Sometimes the truth hurts. There's no way around it. But that doesn't mean we shouldn't tell it. It just may take a while for the person to get past the hurt and see the truth."

I thought about all the times Hailey had told me something I didn't want to hear, but after I had some distance I usually realized she was right. Hopefully, she'd feel the same way.

Mom came over to me, smoothed my hair back, and squeezed my shoulders. "Let's just see how it goes. Hailey's not one to hold a grudge. She adores you. Sometimes friends bug each other. It's part of the deal when you're so close."

"Okay," I said. "I guess so."

We got into the car and drove over to Hailey's. Mom gave a little beep and Hailey came running out. She had just showered, and her hair was still wet and spiky and her cheeks all rosy. She'd even dressed up a bit, which Hailey hardly ever did. She wore a pretty turquoise sweater and her good jeans. She looked great. I waved from the car and smiled, and she waved and smiled back. Good sign. She climbed into the backseat.

"How are you?" I said as Mom started to drive again.

"Good," she said. "Mrs. Martone, thanks for the ride."

"My pleasure," said Mom, and we drove for a minute in silence. Then Mom asked Hailey about soccer and they got into a big conversation about how some of the away games had been going and which other schools had the best teams and so forth. I was relieved Hailey and I didn't have to make awkward conversation the whole time. I checked and made sure I had my notebook so I could jot down some notes during the play.

When we go to the high school, lots of people were gathered outside the auditorium.

"Wow," Mom said. "A great turnout!" The drama club plays are always a big deal, but it seemed like the entire town was here.

"Yeah!" Hailey said.

We walked in, and my mom went to stand in line and pick up the tickets she had already ordered.

I decided to just come out with it. "I'm sorry. I didn't want to hurt your feelings."

"It's okay. I'm sorry if I overreacted. I guess I got carried away with the Michael stuff."

"No, never," I said, joking.

"To tell you the truth, I've been a little jealous."

"Jealous? Jealous of what? My endless crush on Michael Lawrence that never seems to go anywhere?"

"Yeah, kind of. I mean, I've just never felt that way about a guy."

"What about Scott? What about Danny?" I asked, mentioning her past crushes.

"I don't even know what those were. And I'm not really friends with them anymore—I mean, not good friends. Even if you and Michael aren't exactly dating, you have a real friendship. Other than me, he's practically your best friend." She looked down. I was afraid she might even start crying.

"Hailey, why didn't you tell me you felt this way before?"

"Sometimes it's hard to tell the truth," she said, glancing up at me and looking guilty.

"Ah, yeah, just a little," I said, and we both started laughing.

"Michael and I may be friends, but you're in a class by yourself!" I said, and we hugged.

My mom walked back from the ticket line and saw us hugging.

"Wish I had my camera," she said. "I got the tickets; let's go."

We walked into the auditorium. It was going to be a full house. People were everywhere, and more people kept walking in. There was so much buzz and energy. I wondered what Allie was doing right now. Hopefully, she was taking a lot of deep breaths. Even though she had been hard to take lately, I couldn't believe she had the guts to sing and dance in front of all these people. I could never do it. When Hailey slid past me to get to her seat, Mom touched me on the shoulder and smiled. "See, you guys just needed a little time," she whispered. I nodded.

We had great seats—third row, center. We arranged our coats and got comfortable. Then the lights went down. A hush fell over the crowd.

The director came onstage and stood in front of the curtain. "Good evening," he said. "Welcome to our drama club's performance of *West Side Story*. Please shut off all cell phones, cameras, and video devices. Most important, enjoy the show!"

The lights went down again and the curtain went up. A big number for guys was first. The dancing was great and the outfits popped against the multicolored lighting. There was a huge backdrop of a New York cityscape behind them. The dancers leaped around fake fire escapes. It was like a real Broadway show. Allie came on a little later, in a big dance number. She was fantastic. I was so proud of her. I looked at my mom and she was a little misty, like she gets when she's really, really happy. My sister dances like nobody's business.

In fact, Allie was a lot better than Julia Gowen, who played Maria. Julia's first number was strong, but her second wasn't so great. She tripped once on a fake fire escape while dancing, and her voice cracked in a song. Then, after that, she forgot her lines, it seemed to me, about three times during the show. She would suddenly became silent, and the guy who played the male lead, Tony, would whisper in her ear. It was pretty bad. Then, toward the end of the show, there was this huge crash offstage. It was hard to tell exactly where it came from, and the audience was so busy craning their necks to see what had made such a loud noise that they didn't really pay attention to the scene. Plus there were a few weird prop problems. At one point, one of the fake fire escapes wouldn't wheel off the stage and just sat there in the middle of the next scene. The lighting went dark on certain characters, and spotlights would show up on the ceiling.

So, needless to say, the play had some problems. The drama club is great, but I think they might have gotten in a little over their heads with this one.

"Did you like it?" I asked Hailey while we waited for Allie to emerge from backstage.

"Yeah, but it was a little rusty in places. Did you hear that crash?" she asked, her eyes wide and excited.

"Yeah. Well, at least no one got hurt. At least I hope not." It wasn't easy pulling off a production like this, I thought. *School Play Opens, Everyone Survives.* Sheesh. "How about when

Maria forgot her line and Tony had to practically yell it across the stage?" I said. I hoped it was only opening-night jitters and they'd pull it together tomorrow.

"I know," said Hailey, giggling.

Allie came out, still wearing her stage makeup and her eyelashes. Lots of people came up to her and told her she was amazing. She was. I was glad to see her getting the attention she deserved after all her hard work. I saw Julia Gowen too, but it seemed that not as many people were surrounding her. At one point she walked over to where Allie was standing and kind of took over the crowd. Allie finally left her admirers and came over to us with a sour expression on her face. I gave her a huge hug and told her she'd rocked it.

"Thanks, sis," she said, brightening up again.

"Do you have time to come with us for ice cream before your cast party? We want to celebrate with you!" Mom said.

"Sure," Allie said. "Let's go."

At the ice-cream parlor, we gave Allie lots more kudos. She beamed.

"But Julia Gowen was a bit of a disaster. Memorize your lines much?" Allie said while she took a huge spoonful from the brownie sundae Hailey and I were sharing. I waved her hand away.

"Eat your own," I said, pointing to the dish of double chocolate chip in front of her.

"Allie," Mom said, "that's not nice. Maybe Julia just had an off night."

"Well, it's not like Julia Gowen was that nice to me. She was competing with me the whole time, giving me critiques of my numbers when that's supposed to be, like, the director's job. Did you see how she totally took over my moment outside after the show? During rehearsals, she waltzed around like she was a Broadway diva instead of in a local school play. I mean, seriously, who acts like that?"

"I can't imagine," Mom said, and gave me a secret smile.

"It's just because she knows you should have gotten the part of Maria. She's just insecure," Hailey said, her mouth stuffed with ice cream and brownie.

"There's a reason I've always liked you," Allie said to Hailey with a wink. Then they high-fived. Oh boy, now I was starting to feel a little sick, and it wasn't because of all that ice cream.

The next morning I jumped out of bed. Today was the day before the night of my almost first date with Michael Lawrence. How was I going to eat? What was I going to wear? I couldn't do this alone. I was so glad Hailey and I had figured things out, because I didn't think I'd get through this day without her.

After breakfast I called her.

"I need outfit advice," I cried when she answered the phone.

"I'll be over in an hour," she replied, and hung up.

Mom let me use her digital camera so we could take pictures of each outfit I tried on. We pulled out a bunch of choices from my closet. Long skirts, short skirts, jeans and blouses, scarves, everything I had that would possibly be almost Saturday-night dateworthy. We played music and did rounds of combinations, and Hailey took pictures of all my looks. Then we downloaded them on the computer.

We were looking at two pictures side by side on my computer screen, comparing a pink embroidered T-shirt with a long gray skirt to skinny jeans and my silky green tunic, when there was a thud at the door.

"What are you guys doing in here?" Allie said frantically when we opened the door. "I can't hear myself sing!"

That would probably be a first.

"You don't want to wear yourself out. You still have two more shows," I said, in the nicest possible way I could. I really didn't want to set Allie off now. She had two shows today, one in a couple of hours.

"I know," Allie said, sitting down on my bed and heaving a big sigh. "Maybe you're right."

I'm *right*? Did Allie just say I'm right? I wish I could have recorded it.

"So what's going on?" Allie demanded, getting up again and examining the clothes that were thrown everywhere, picking up the silky pale pink T-shirt with the flower embroidered in the same color on the front.

"Is this mine?" she said. Before I could answer, she went on. "Wait a minute . . . wait a minute, I know what's going on here. You're going to the play tonight with Michael Lawrence!" she said, and poked me in the chest.

I turned beet red. Hailey looked at me and back at Allie, opened her mouth to say something, and then seemed to think better of it.

"It's just a . . . thing for the paper," I said, shrugging. Now I completely regretted mentioning this to her casually the other night after dinner. Allie hadn't teased me for it then, probably because she was so wrapped up in rehearsals, but now I had a feeling she was going to make up for lost time.

Allie had a big smirk on her face. "Yeah, just a thing. Uh-huh."

"Whatever, Allie. You're in a different mood

every other second, and you haven't been that nice to any of us. I know the play is a lot of work, but it has kind of, well"—I thought for a moment, both Hailey and Allie staring at me, waiting for what I would say next—"taken over your life. And not always in a good way. So if you're going to be obnoxious about it, just leave us alone." There! I'd said it. I wasn't afraid of Allie's reaction, either. She needed to hear it. I glanced at Hailey, and her mouth was hanging open. She quickly closed it. At first Allie looked surprised; then a little hurt; then her face softened.

"Show me your top outfits. We'll get you looking so good, Michael won't be able to pay attention to the show," she said as she started holding up shirts against me.

My shoulders relaxed. Maybe she'd actually heard me for once. "And you promise you're not going to freak out and starting screaming at us about something?" I asked her.

"Just as long as you don't upstage me!" she said, and we laughed, but I think she might have only been half joking.

I tried on the top two outfits again. Allie chose the green tunic and skinny jeans, but added my brown suede boots, silver hoops, and a silky gray scarf. She stood back.

"Wear your hair down," she said. "And wait!" She ran out of the room and came back with a clear lip gloss and smoothed it on me. "Perfect!"

"You look awesome," said Hailey.

"Thanks," I said, suddenly feeling shy with both of them admiring me. I turned around to check myself out in the mirror. *Not bad, Martone*, I thought. ***Frazzled Reporter Cleans Up Nice.***

Chapter 9

ARTS REPORTER HAS NERVOUS BREAKDOWN AT THEATER

★ ★ ★

"Sammy!" my mother called from the kitchen. "Let's go. Don't want you to be late for your big night!"

I came out in my outfit, lip gloss shining and sticky on my mouth.

"Wow," she said. "You look so cute!"

I smiled and blushed a bit, but I was kind of hoping for more than "cute." Oh well, she was my mom. We headed out to the car and drove once again to the high school auditorium.

"So, are you excited?" she asked me.

"About the play?" I asked back.

"No, silly, about going to the play with Michael!"

"Please, Mom. It's just something we have to do for the paper," I said for the hundredth time. Maybe the more I said it, the more I'd believe it.

"Oh, okay," she said, and didn't say another word until we were almost there. I gazed down the long street that ran past the school and could see the crowds gathering in front of the auditorium entrance. It looked even more crowded than it had on opening night.

"Mom, can you just drop me off here?" I said in a rushed tone, feeling the nervousness take over my body. My hands felt shaky and my stomach started doing backflips.

"Really, this far away?" she said.

"It's okay, I don't mind walking," I said, smoothing my hair. Now I was starting to feel sweaty.

She gave me a quick hug. "You look gorgeous," she said. "Have a great time."

"Thanks, Mom." I know she meant it, too.

I got out of the car, walked down the sidewalk toward the auditorium, and stood at the front doors, watching people greet each other and head inside.

Should I wait out here? I wondered. Should I go in and wait there? Maybe I should find someone I knew to talk to so I didn't look like I was actually waiting. But wasn't that what I was supposed to be doing, waiting for Michael? *Arts Reporter Has Nervous Breakdown at Theater.* Stranger things have happened.

Just as I was about to go inside, thinking that somehow I'd seem less awkward in the lobby, Michael came jogging up to me, smiling.

"Okay, Take Two—the second time in one day!" he said cheerfully. He looked so good in khakis and a crisp white button-down shirt with the sleeves rolled up that I suddenly couldn't move my mouth.

"You look great," he said.

A flash of warmth spread over me. "Thanks, so do you," I said in a strange tiny voice. *Sam, keep it together. This is a newspaper assignment, NOT a date*, I tried to tell myself. "So, let's get our seats!" I blurted out, and started walking.

We both had our tickets and headed straight into the auditorium to sit down. I hadn't remembered the seats being so close to one another. I crossed my legs, trying not to brush against Michael's by accident. We chatted about the performances we had seen earlier, and then the lights went down. Suddenly I was sitting in the dark, four inches apart from Michael Lawrence. I could hear him breathing. I could even smell the Tide detergent scent on his clothes. It was almost too much.

The opening act started, and Michael took out a little notebook. I did the same. He was sitting to the left of me, and he laid his right arm on the armrest between us. His arm was now an inch away from me. The lady to my right had her arm on her left armrest. Suddenly all I could think about was Michael's arm so close to me and where in the world I was going to put my hands. I scrunched them in my lap and held the notebook on my thigh.

Well into the second act, I noticed Michael lifting his arms up and stretching. Okay, now I had a little room to stretch out too. Then Michael put his arm on the armrest again and brushed against my arm. I felt electricity shoot through me. Was that on purpose or by accident? I gave him a glance out of the corner of my eye. He was staring straight ahead. I quickly switched my gaze forward. How was I going to concentrate on the play? Now I was in a full sweat. Perfect. I'll bet professional arts reviewers don't have to deal with these things.

Somehow I managed to pay some attention to the rest of the play. Allie was great, as usual, but Julia Gowen seemed as off as she had been the first night. One part of the city backdrop kept falling down, and they still had problems with the spotlights. Maybe I was being too critical? At least I was reviewing the play with Michael and we could compare notes.

At the end, the cast came out for a bow, and the crowd went crazy. I yelled, "Go, Allie!" and Michael did too, even louder than me, which I thought was a bit strange. It was the last performance, and I could see relief on the director's face as he came out for his bow. I watched Allie bask in her final moment as Anita and I wondered how she felt. Was she happy that it was finally over and she hadn't messed up any lines or dance moves, at least as far as I could tell? Or did she feel kind of sad that it was over, along with all the excitement and the attention that came with it? That's kind of how I felt after a big story of mine ran in the *Voice*. But I also felt happy that it was done. *I* certainly was glad the play was over. I'm happy Allie did such a great job, but it would have been nice not to be trying to sleep while she belted out "America" in the next room.

As the lights came on and we stood up, Michael and I looked at each other. Now what? I heard Hailey's voice in my ear: *Let him fill in the blanks.* I smiled and kept my mouth shut. Michael smiled back and started walking out. I followed. He stopped when we were outside. People were everywhere—coming out, getting into cars, yelling out plans to each other.

"How'd you like it?" I asked him. I had to say something.

"It was okay. Pretty similar to the matinee. So, um, want to go to Slices and talk it over? I'm starving."

"Oh, sure. Definitely." I nervously started

playing with the little tassels at the end of my scarf. Now did this count as an official date? I had to restrain myself from calling Hailey right then and there. I texted my mom, and she texted right back "Have fun!" with a smiley face. Mom seemed just as excited as Hailey.

We walked over to Slices Pizzeria, the most popular local pizza joint in our town. Their pizza was popular for a reason. The crust was superthin and crispy, and the secret recipe for the incredible marinara was said to be kept in a safe, according to Leo, the owner. When we walked in, I looked around, and I swear half our school was stuffed in there. It hadn't occurred to me that we probably wouldn't be the only people getting a slice after the show. I saw some of the guys from the baseball team at the same table, sharing a pie.

"Hey, man!" Jamal Williams said, high-fiving Michael as we walked past. Then he waved hi to me. A couple of other guys at the table did the same. I waved back.

"What are you guys up to?" Jamal asked, with a twinkle in his eye. Everyone at the table was suddenly listening really hard. Michael and I glanced at each other.

"Oh, we're just working," he said casually. "Sam and I are reviewing the play for the paper, so we need to hang out and compare notes."

My heart dropped to my shoes. "Just working" is what he said. Suddenly I felt stupid in my fancy scarf and earrings and lip gloss. Is that all this meant to him? I guess even being asked to a pizzeria didn't count as a date. We left the guys and went up to the counter. We each ordered a slice and a Sprite. I pulled out a ten-dollar bill Mom had given me in case we went out for something to eat after the play.

"No, no," Michael said, "I got it," and he handed the cashier his money before I could even say a word.

"Thanks! You didn't have to do that," I said, surprised and even more confused. Wasn't I supposed to know if this was a date or not? I had answered that Dear Know-It-All letter so sure of myself. If he asks you to something or if you ask him to something, it's a date.

But what if you ask him to the first part and then he asks you to the second part? What if he tells his friends it's just for the paper but *then* he offers to pay? *Boy Causes Case of Permanent Date Confusion. Girl Never Recovers.* We finally found a little table in the back and sat down. I took out my notes, and Michael did too.

"The show was pretty good, but kind of the same as opening night," I said, happy to get my mind off date stuff and just think about the review. "I mean, a lot of work went into it. The sets and lighting were pretty elaborate. Some of the performers were great. Some were not so great."

"I agree. I don't know about Julia Gowen. She has a nice voice, but she just never seemed comfortable up there, at least not tonight."

"How about the matinee? Was she any better?" I asked.

"Not really," Michael said, and took a sip of soda.

"Yeah, she was kind of the same at opening night. I thought it might just be jitters. Guess not." I took a tiny bite of pizza, hoping I wouldn't get any sauce on my face.

"Your sister was great, though!" Michael said, suddenly excited. "She's, like, really awesome."

For crying out loud. This was not what I wanted to hear on my sort of date/not date with Michael Lawrence—how fabulous my sister was. I hoped—no, I prayed with every bone in my body—that he didn't have a crush on her. That would make me just want to move out of town. Tonight.

After we finished our pizza, Michael suggested ice cream. This time I offered to pay and he accepted. More date confusion. We got cones, him a rocky road, me a caramel vanilla swirl, and sat outside on a bench, eating them. We were quiet for a moment. The night was really clear and still; no wind at all. It wasn't too hot or cold outside, just perfect spring weather.

"Look at the sky," Michael said, tilting back his head.

I tilted my head back. It was an inky blue, each star glowing like a rhinestone sprinkled into the atmosphere.

"You can see so many stars," I said. "Magical."

"We used to go to Montana on summer vacations to visit my uncle when he lived there," Michael said. "And the sky looked like this, only bigger and brighter. It was amazing."

"I'll bet. Wish I could have seen it."

"Yeah," Michael said, looking at me. "You should go if you ever have the chance." He cleared his throat and seemed a bit nervous. His cheeks were rosy. He put his arm on the bench behind me and leaned back his head back again to look at the sky. I had already called my mom to tell her to pick me up and she would probably be here any second, but I didn't want to leave this bench. Ever.

"I had fun tonight," I blurted out.

He stopped looking at the sky and stared straight at me. "Me too, Paste."

"Enough with that ridiculous nickname, Mikey," I said. Oof. Way to ruin a moment, Sam.

He seemed truly embarrassed. "Sorry, it's a habit. Me too, *Sam*. Or should I be calling you Samantha?" Before I could answer, my mom pulled up, smiling and waving. I asked him if he wanted a ride home.

"Sure," he said. "That would be great."

He hopped into the backseat, while I sat in front with my mom. We discussed the play, more of its good points and bad. Michael told my mom how great Allie was *again* and I rolled my eyes in the dark. After we dropped him off, Mom turned to me.

"So, how was it? You're grinning from ear to ear," she said.

"It was good," I said, trying to hide my smile.

"You pick 'em well, Sam."

"Mom," I said, rolling my eyes. "It was just for the paper. I told you!"

"Sure, honey, just for the paper," Mom said, and gave me a wink.

I couldn't help but laugh. As much as I tried to keep my cover, the night definitely felt like more than that. If it talks like a date and walks like date, it's a date, right?

Chapter 10

ADVISOR OF SCHOOL NEWSPAPER RUINS GREAT ROMANCE!

★ ★ ★

"Sam, it's Hailey. You awake?" my mom asked softly at eight thirty the next morning, standing next to my bed and holding the phone.

I rolled over. I kind of was, barely. "Uh-huh" was all I could say, and took it from her.

"Mmm?" I said.

"Well?" Hailey's voice burst through the phone. She's much more of a morning person than I am. I think it's because she's used to getting up early sometimes for practices and games. Me, I hardly roll out of bed before ten on a Sunday morning. But not this Sunday, apparently.

"Whatever could you be talking about?" I said playfully, rubbing my eyes. "And why did you call me so early, Hailey?"

"That good, huh? Why didn't you text me last night?"

"Sorry, got home late. Crashed," I said, yawning.

"Spill it," she said.

I told her about the whole night, the thing Michael said at Slices about "just working." Then I told her that he'd asked me to have pizza and paid, and about the ice cream and how I paid. I kept the stargazing to myself. It was the best part, but for some reason I was afraid that if I explained it, it would sound goofy, or would just seem less special.

"That's totally a date," she said.

"You think? I never know with Michael. And I feel like he might have a thing for Allie, which makes me nauseous if I think about it too long," I said in a lower voice, although Allie would probably sleep until noon this morning, since she was recovering from the play and from cast parties on both nights.

"No! Really?" Hailey said. I told her what Michael had said after the play.

"That doesn't mean anything," she said. "I thought Allie was awesome too. Everyone did."

She was probably right and I was worrying for nothing. After I got off the phone with Hailey, I went down for breakfast. As I was digging into a delicious plate of waffles, strawberries, and a bit of vanilla yogurt on top, the phone rang again. Mom answered it and handed it to me.

"Michael," she said in a hushed tone, a bit of excitement hidden in her voice.

Everyone was up this morning! I got a fluttery feeling in my stomach and cleared my throat, before grabbing the phone and taking it into the den for privacy.

"Hi," I said.

"Hi, Pasty," he said, loud and energized. Great, we were back to nicknames. "We need to figure out when we're going to meet and write this thing. It's due Friday."

"I know. How about tomorrow after school?" I asked.

"Sure. Can it be a little later, like four thirty? I have practice. Want to meet me back at my house?"

"Only if you make your amazing cinnamon buns," I said.

"Sure, just for you, Snacky," he said. I laughed. Maybe the nicknames were okay. He didn't call anyone else these things, ridiculous as they were.

When I got there the next day, right at four thirty, Michael's mom let me in. The house smelled so good. How did he even have time to bake cinnamon buns after practice? I was touched that he had gone the extra mile for me.

I went into the kitchen. Michael had oven mitts on, looking as cute as can be as he took a couple of buns out of the toaster oven.

"I keep a few in the freezer, in case I ever have a Snacky emergency such as this one," he said.

Did he really keep cinnamon buns in the freezer for me? I knew I was blushing. "They smell terrific, as usual," I said. "In fact, I wish I could just bottle the smell and spray it on as perfume whenever I get into that cinnamon-bun-craving mood."

He laughed, got two plates, and put a bun on each. Then he poured two glasses of milk and brought them to the table. No matter what happened with Michael, he was a good friend.

After we'd scarfed down our snacks, we started outlining the article.

"Okay, so I wrote this checklist about all the areas we want to cover," I said, showing Michael my list and the notes I had taken during the two shows.

"Of course you did, Listy," he said.

"Ha-ha."

"But wait," he said, looking more closely at my notes. "I wrote that the scenery fell down in act two on Saturday night."

I took my notebook back and read over what I'd written. "But it says that the scenery fell during the first big dance number. So that had to be during act one."

Michael checked over his notes. "It definitely fell during the song 'America' in the matinee."

"That was act one," I said, flipping the pages back and forth in my notebook. I was suddenly worried that I hadn't taken careful enough notes. And what if Michael hadn't either?

"Do you think it matters?" Michael said, sitting back in his chair.

"Do I think what matters?" I asked.

"Which act this stuff happened in?"

"This is how I see it," I said, trying to muster up some confidence while wiping a bit of icing off my chin. "We're going to have to be critical, no way around it. There were a lot of mistakes. Too many, in my opinion, for a drama club that has won so many awards and has such a strong reputation. Trust me, it would be easier if we could just say everything's great. But if we are going to pick it apart . . ."

". . . then we'd better be accurate," Michael said, reading my mind.

"Exactly," I said, and smiled. "I might need another cinnamon bun to get through this."

"Coming right up," he said, and went to the freezer.

That night I looked over what we had. We still couldn't agree on when certain mistakes happened, based on our notes. I wasn't sure how we were going to figure it out before Friday.

I couldn't ask Allie. She'd freak out knowing I was actually going to write about these things. I lay down on my bed and stared at the ceiling, exhausted. I guess writing a play review isn't so simple after all.

The next day we met right after school in the *Voice* office. We started drafting the beginning so we'd have at least something down.

"How are we going to fact-check this stuff?" I said, running my hands through my hair. I was starting to get stressed out. It was already Tuesday and we weren't much closer to a finished piece than we were yesterday.

Michael leaned back in his chair and chewed on the end of his pencil. It's something he likes to do when he's thinking. I noticed that all his pencils had little bite marks around the erasers. He suddenly leaned forward and pointed his pencil at me.

"Of course! The school always records DVDs of the shows and keeps them in the library. We can fact-check that way," he said.

"Right!" I said, equally excited, but then thought about our time constraints and slumped in my chair. "That's going to take a long time, going through all that footage for each performance," I said. "How are we going to get it done in time?"

"I think we need to get busy. What are you doing tonight?" he asked me.

"Nothing," I said.

"Great, it's a date!" he added.

I looked up from my notebook, surprised.

"I—I mean, you know, as an expression," he backpedaled, and then started nibbling on his pencil again.

"Yeah, of course," I said hurriedly. "I knew you meant it that way." But I wondered if he *knew* he meant it that way.

"But you know, maybe some other time, we . . ." And then he stopped.

"We what?" I asked, my heart suddenly racing.

Then the door swung open and there was Mr. Trigg. He put down a stack of books he was carrying and plugged in his electric teapot. Aarrgh! *Advisor of School Newspaper Ruins Great Romance!*

"Cheers, fellow journos! How's my modern Woodward-and-Bernstein team doing?" he said while getting his tea things together. In a moment he would offer us some tea, and then we'd be stuck here with Mr. Trigg in the middle for at least another ten minutes.

Michael and I quickly glanced at each other. I stood up and started clearing my stuff quickly. Michael started to do the same.

"We're great, but I just forgot something that I have to do," I said, and went to the door. My head was about to burst.

"Yeah, me too. We have to get to the library before it closes," Michael said quickly.

"Right! That's absolutely right!" I said loudly. Both Michael and Mr. Trigg looked at me, seeming alarmed.

"You okay?" Michael asked.

I nodded. "So I guess we'd better go," I tried to say more calmly.

"Um, yeah. See ya later, Mr. Trigg," Michael said.

Mr. Trigg gave us a salute and we both hurried out the door. We rushed down the hall. "I'm glad you remembered that. What time is it? The library closes at four."

"It's exactly four!" he cried.

The library was on the other side of the school. We made a left and ran down another hallway. When we got to the end, we saw that the janitor had blocked off the next hallway for cleaning.

"Follow me!" Michael called out, turning around and going back to where we'd come from and down another hallway. Now we had to go the long way around. I followed as fast as I could, but the floor was slippery and I certainly didn't want to have a wipeout now. We arrived at the library, breathless, just as Mrs. Osborne, the librarian, was coming out.

"Wait!" Michael called to her.

"Please! We have a library emergency!" I said, catching up.

She glanced over her shoulder slowly as she was turning the key in the lock of the library door.

She seemed tired. Her bag looked heavy on her shoulder, and her glasses were slipping down her nose. I hadn't really thought about it before, but maybe it was hard to be a librarian, with kids asking you questions all day long.

"Tomorrow's another day, folks," she said, going back to her lock and key.

We both stood in front of her and started to explain our problem, right at the same time, loudly.

"Whoa, whoa! Slow down. You need the DVD for *West Side Story*?"

"The school production," Michael and I both said at the same time.

"So we can fact-check for our review," I said.

"That's due this Friday," Michael said. Now we were filling in each other's sentences.

Mrs. Osborne grumbled something I couldn't hear, and then she got her keys out of her pocket.

"You have two minutes to find it," she said, and opened the door.

We yelled out thank-yous and fled to the dark DVD section, since the lights were all off. We ran our eyes over the cases, which were arranged alphabetically. Luckily, it wasn't a huge section. If someone had the DVD out already, or if they hadn't put it in the library yet, we were toast.

"Here!" Michael said, holding up a red case. On the front was a picture of the cast. I saw Allie's smiling face near the middle of the lineup. We ran back to the counter, and Mrs. Osborne checked it out quickly. We all walked out together.

"We appreciate it, Mrs. Osborne," I said in my sweetest tone.

"Well, write a good review," she said. She hauled her bag over her shoulder and went down the hall.

"Man, that was lucky," Michael said when we got outside.

"Yeah. So what time tonight?"

"Maybe seven?" I said.

"Great, see you later," he said, and we walked off in our different directions.

Chapter 11

BOY ASKS GIRL TO WATCH MOVIE AT UNKNOWN LOCATION

Back home that afternoon, I realized we never actually said whose house we were going to. I figured that since Michael had asked, it would probably be his, but I didn't want to just show up at his house without making sure. I didn't know if I should call him or wait for him to call me. *Boy Asks Girl to Watch Movie at Unknown Location.* What I really wanted to know was what he had planned to say to me before Mr. Trigg burst in and ruined it all. I knocked on Allie's door. She had calmed down since sleeping practically all day Sunday. When Allie was in a decent mood, she gave me good boy advice. She was almost normal last night at dinner. She didn't even get mad or sing or try to text her friends.

"Yeah?" she called.

"It's me. Boy trouble," I said, knowing that would get her going.

I could hear the springs in her bed creak as she bounded up to answer the door.

"Trouble in paradise?" she said, grinning.

We both flopped down on her bed, me lying on my stomach at the foot, my face held up by my hands, Allie propping herself up with pillows at the head.

"Not much of a paradise, and if you make fun of me, I'm not going to tell you anything," I said, raising my head and glaring at her.

"Okay, okay. It's just so tempting. But seriously, what's going on?"

I told her about Michael asking me to meet him tonight, but not exactly asking me over.

"I mean, do I show up at his house at seven? What if that's presumptuous? Should I call?"

Allie chewed on her thumbnail as she thought for a moment, then shook her head. "No, he asked you. That means it's at his house. You're overthinking things, as usual," she said. "Now, I've got a ton of homework—I'm still catching up on everything I didn't do last week because of the play. So skedaddle." She waved at me.

"Well, nice spending this quality time with you," I said, getting up and walking toward the door.

"Anytime," Allie called as I closed her door.

I went into my room, sat on my desk chair, and took a few spins. That always calmed me. I checked out some of my favorite news blogs and looked at the clock. It was only five thirty. I tried to do my math homework, but could hardly concentrate and kept staring at the clock. Even though Allie's talk was short and sweet, I think she was right. I wanted another opinion, so I thought of e-mailing Hailey, but I kind of wanted to leave her alone for a while with all my Michael stuff. I can understand that when your love life hasn't been that interesting, you might not want to hear about someone else's. Then, like a beacon in the night, an IM blinked on the screen.

Can we watch at ur house? Parents r having friends over for dnr.

No problemo! I zinged back a half a second later.

Thank goodness. Problem solved!

I asked my mom if Michael could come over, knowing she would be fine with it, and rushed through our dinner. Mom said there was ice cream for dessert, or we could make popcorn.

When Michael knocked on the door, Allie came flying out of nowhere and was opening it before I'd even gotten up from my seat.

"Hello there," she said, all sparkly, flipping her hair from one shoulder to another.

Michael gave her a big smile. He looked so cute in jeans and a gray hoodie.

"Hi, Allie. You were so good in the play!" he said, stuffing his hands in his pockets.

And then I saw it. My sister blushed. I felt sort of sick. "You'd better give me a good review," she said, batting her eyes at him.

He just nodded.

"So, Michael, we'd better get started," I said,

giving my sister the evil eye.

"What? Oh, yeah! Sure!" he said, looking embarrassed. He grabbed his backpack and followed me into the den.

The rest of the night went well. We watched the Friday night performance and the Saturday matinee. We clarified most of our notes. The scenery definitely fell both times in the first act. We made popcorn and Allie and Mom joined us for a bit, but then we couldn't discuss any of the play's problems in front of Allie. I just recorded them in my notes. Anyway, Allie was so enthralled by her own performance, she didn't seem to care that I was taking notes. I stole glances at Michael when Allie was singing her big number onstage. He was watching a little too closely, I thought. It got late quickly and we decided to watch the last show the next day.

"So now you forget all about me because you're busy with the paper . . . and Michael again?"

Hailey said while I was stuffing books in my locker with my foot the next morning.

"Never, my dear, dear Hailey—you are unforgettable!" I said. I took her by the hands, twirled, and dipped her. Then we both kind of klutzed out and landed in a heap on the floor, giggling.

"Want the truth?" I asked, promising myself I'd be really direct with Hailey. She got up and pulled me to my feet.

"Always, you know that," she said, but she didn't look at me. Suddenly she was really busy with her locker.

I took a deep breath. "I didn't want to bug you with too much Michael stuff. I just know you might not want to hear about it every day. We've been pushing to get the play review done. That and Michael are all I'm kind of thinking about right now." I watched her carefully to see if she was taking it okay.

She turned to me. "It's fine, I understand. And I always want to hear about Michael stuff. It's never boring to me," she said, and she seemed to mean it.

I relaxed my shoulders and smiled. I knew that I could always count on Hailey.

"How about a girls' night this Friday after I turn in my pieces for the *Voice*? We could rent a movie, do our nails. You could sleep over?"

"Yay!" Hailey said, and clapped her hands. Then her faced scrunched up. "But I thought you were just writing the review. What's the other piece?"

I froze. I hadn't meant to say "pieces," but I was thinking about the review and the Dear Know-It-All letter that was also looming. So dumb. "'Pieces'? I meant 'piece.' This review has suddenly become such a bear, it seems like more than one!" I said, trying to sound believable.

"All that time with Michael is just messing with your head," she said.

That night I went to Michael's to watch the last show. I realized when I got there that I was just wearing jeans and a T-shirt, and nothing fancy. It's funny—when I spend a lot of time with Michael, I don't think about what I'm wearing and what I look like when I'm eating pizza or popcorn anymore. We just hang out and have a good time, like two regular people. I wonder if that's how it is when you have a boyfriend. Maybe a little of both? I can't wait for this review to be done, but in some ways I don't want it to be. Then we'll have to go back to bumping into each other in the cafeteria—literally, if Hailey has anything to do with it.

On Thursday afternoon we met in Trigger's office to finally lay it all out. We combined our notes, did a draft, and then I typed it up. We started off in a positive light and wrote about the long history of stellar performances by the drama club. We talked about all the strong singing and dancing, especially Allison Martone's excellent portrayal of Anita; the complicated staging; and the ambitious lighting and scenery. Then we got down to business and mentioned the "inconsistent performance" by Julia Gowen and some of the other key players. We also got into details about the lighting mishaps and the scenery disasters. We couldn't help but mention the huge crash that was a cause of distraction and concern on Friday night. We ended by saying that even with all the mishaps, "the run was still a showcase of theatrical talent that our town has become accustomed to, but the drama club might be served better by a simpler choice of play." I felt like our review was honest, accurate, and well supported. That's all a critic could do, right?

"And scene," I announced as I typed the last word. We stood up and gave each other a double high five, which became a quick hug. I couldn't believe I was hugging Michael Lawrence. I breathed in the Tide and then snapped back to the real world. Michael must have felt the same way, because suddenly we pulled away from each other.

"Okay, so I've got to run. Practice in fifteen minutes!" he said, his face a bit red as he grabbed his things and packed up.

"Yeah, me too," I said, even though I wasn't in any rush at all.

"But wait," Michael said, sitting down, running his fingers through his hair. He looked troubled.

"What is it?" I said, scared of what he was about

to say. Maybe it was about how unprofessional it was for us to hug.

"Are we being too harsh? It's not a favorable review. I mean, what about your sister? Won't she be upset?"

"My sister?" I said, my mouth dropping open. "First of all, we totally complimented her performance. Second of all, who cares about Allie? She didn't direct the play. We justified all our criticisms. We are reporters, after all, and it's up to us to be professional, unbiased, and not influenced by"—I was becoming slightly hysterical now, waving my hands around—"by people's sisters!" I knew it. He just wanted to be close to me because he had a crush on Allie!

"Okay, okay. Calm down," he said, looking down at the table. "I guess you're right. And it's your sister, not mine."

"That's right, she's *my* sister," I said, not really sure of what, exactly, I meant.

After we posted the piece online in deathly quiet, we rushed out of the office and went our separate ways.

★   ★   ★

On Friday night, while Hailey and I were doing facial masks, we went over everything in full detail. Hailey lay on my bed, her face covered in green paste. I was on the floor, also looking like I'd gotten carried away with toothpaste.

Hailey said, "He doesn't have a crush on Allie any more than any seventh grader would on a pretty high school girl. I mean, he's human."

"So you're on his side?" I said, getting slightly peeved.

"Duh, of course not. I'm just giving you some perspective and being honest. What about the ice cream and the hug and making popcorn and all that's happened between you guys the last couple of weeks? But then again, maybe you're right—I mean, how could he have a crush on you when you look like that?" she said, giggling.

We both went to the mirror and looked at our strange alien faces and laughed. When we laughed, the dried masks cracked all over, making us look even stranger and causing more fits of laughter. This was exactly what I needed, just a silly night with my bestie. *Medical Research Shows Sleepovers with Best Friends a Cure-All.*

"No more boy talk tonight," I said when we recovered. Hailey was probably right, anyway. "Deal?"

"Deal," she said.

Since I'd been so wrapped up with the review, which had taken longer to write than some of our other pieces, I told Mr. Trigg I was just going to answer a letter I had gotten a while ago for the column. A guy—I think it was a guy—wrote in about wanting to spend more time with his busy dad, but didn't know how to ask. I basically told him he just needed to be honest and direct and tell his dad how he felt, because maybe his dad didn't even know. I didn't really this know from experience, since my dad died when I was really little and I don't remember him much, but my mom is always busy, since she's sort of the mom and the dad of our family. Sometimes I have to ask for special time with her, and she always thanks me for telling her how I feel.

Chapter 12

INNOCENT REPORTER GETS AMBUSHED

★ ★ ★

The next few days at school went by pretty quietly. I felt much better since having some nice quality time with Hailey to ground me. I hadn't spoken to or seen Michael, but that was okay. Maybe we had spent too much time together. I wasn't even mad anymore about Allie. I just wanted to forget the whole thing.

Later in the afternoon, I went to my locker to get stuff for my last class. A seventh grader I barely knew, Todd Gibbons, who worked backstage for the play, came walking straight up to me.

"You shouldn't criticize something you know nothing about," he said.

"Excuse me?" I said, unsure of what he was talking about.

"The review. I mean, who do you guys think you are? We worked hard on that show," he said, and walked away, shaking his head.

I got a sinking feeling in my stomach. No one had ever reacted like this to one of my articles for the paper. Maybe Todd Gibbons was just extra-sensitive or having a bad day. I grabbed my backpack and headed toward class. As I walked down the hall, at least three people glared at me. I hurried to class and slipped into my seat in the middle of the classroom.

During class, a note was flung onto my desk. I didn't see where it came from. I looked around, but no one was looking at me. Then I saw Katie Minor, a drama club member who was one of the dancers in the play, turn toward me and then quickly look away. I opened up the note with shaky hands.

It said,

Your review was totally biased and completely unfair. The drama club is pretty upset. Way to go.

-Katie

I sat there, gawking at the note. Biased? How was I biased? It would have been biased if we had given it a perfect review because we didn't want to hurt anyone's feelings. Somehow, being "biased" in Katie's mind was honesty to me and Michael. I thought about Too Honest's question, and it was becoming all too apparent to me that people don't want to hear the truth even when they ask for it, and they certainly don't want to hear it when they don't ask, if it's not positive.

The minutes felt like hours as I waited for class to end. When the bell rang, I was the first one out. In the hallway, someone yelled out at me, "If you don't have anything nice to say, then don't say it at all!" **_Innocent Reporter Gets Ambushed._** It seriously felt that way. I didn't look to see who it was, I just hightailed it to the *Voice* office to see if Mr. Trigg was around. I didn't want to be alone with this anymore. It was the end of the day, and Hailey was at soccer practice, which had just started up again. I was tempted to go flag her down, but this wasn't her problem and I didn't want to distract her. I was hoping to see Michael, but I was pretty sure he had practice too. Just my luck—my two closest friends were both athletes. I wondered if Michael had been getting the same treatment.

Taped to the closed door of the office was a note. I took it down and went inside. I kept the lights off and sat in the seat farthest from the door so no one would think I was inside. Mr. Trigg usually stopped by here at the end of the day. At least I wouldn't be roaming the hallways anymore. I read the note:

To the Voice,

We are highly disappointed in the mediocre review Michael Lawrence and Samantha Martone gave our production of West Side Story. We are one of the longest-running drama clubs in the county and have won several prestigious awards and contests. We do expect an unbiased review from our school newspaper, but we believe much of the criticism to be unfair and unfounded. We assumed that as the school newspaper, you would be more supportive to our district's artistic endeavors.

Sincerely,

The Drama Club

I quietly folded the letter in my lap. What had Michael and I been thinking? We weren't professional reviewers. It wasn't our *job*. I was just some kid wannabe reporter who got put on the wrong assignment, obviously. Now I was starting to feel angry at Mr. Trigg. Why hadn't he stopped us from publishing the review?

Just then Mr. Trigg walked in. He flung his scarf over his desk chair, not seeing me, and picked up his teacup.

"Hi," I said in a low tone, hoping I wouldn't startle him.

"Good gravy!" said Mr. Trigg, twisting around and squinting at me, almost dropping his cup. "Ms. Martone? Why are you sitting here with the lights out?"

"Sorry—I needed to talk to you, but I didn't want anyone to see me in here," I said, standing up and handing him the letter from the drama club. "This was taped on the door."

He took the letter from me, slipped his reading glasses out of his pocket, and took a look.

"I see," he murmured. "Yes, the drama club

advisor called me as well. They are not pleased and, in my opinion, taking this way too hard."

"Did we go too far?" I asked quietly.

"Absolutely not," Mr. Trigg said. "This is part of the game. Get out of the kitchen if you can't stand the heat, I say to the drama club!"

"Huh?" Sometimes I had no idea at all what Mr. Trigg was talking about.

He cleared his throat and sat down. "I told her you both backed up your criticism with examples. You went and saw all the performances. It was a fair review, and just an opinion." He took off his glasses and pointed at me with them. "Ms. Martone, I saw the play too, and I agreed with the review. You guys did a great job. A little drama, no pun intended, goes with the territory of being a critic and a performer," he said, finishing his speech. He had a satisfied look on his face, but I wasn't sure about how I felt. I hated to think I made so many people upset—people who had worked hard and had done their best.

I said good-bye to Mr. Trigg, slipped out of school, and slunk home. When I got in, Mom was there in her office, but Allie was out. I couldn't face Allie yet anyway.

"Mom!" I called.

"Hi," she said. "How was your day?"

"Awful," I said, collapsing in the tears I'd been holding. She listened to my story, wiping my tears away with a tissue. I sat on the old orange armchair in her office and held the throw pillow against me.

"Oh, honey. You didn't do anything wrong. They are just being bad sports. The drama club may not be used to getting criticism, but it doesn't mean they never should."

"I guess not," I said, wiping my tears.

"I'll make a nice dinner. We'll relax," she said.

The phone rang and I ran to the den to get it.

"Hi," Michael said after I answered. "Did you get accosted about the review today too?" he asked.

"That's an understatement," I said.

"It comes with the territory," he said. "I get yelled at all the time on the field when I pitch a bad game."

"I'm just not used to being the target of hostility like that," I said.

"What doesn't kill you makes you stronger," Michael replied.

"That's a harsh way of looking at it."

"My dad always says that to me, but I think it's true. Really, don't worry about it. They'll get over it. Just wait a few days."

"Okay, I'll try. Thanks for calling," I told him before hanging up. I was really glad he called. It made me feel less alone. It was also nice to hear his voice after everything we had been through.

I went into the kitchen and helped Mom chop tomatoes and cucumbers for the salad. She put a chicken and potatoes in the oven. Soon the kitchen filled with the comforting aroma of food roasting.

"Mmm, smells good," said Allie, coming through the front door just as dinner was ready. Mom and I were setting the table. I didn't want to face Allie, but maybe it wouldn't be so bad. At least we wrote that she was good.

Allie came into the kitchen, smiling at Mom. Then she gave me a cold stare. I decided not to say anything. Mom put the food on the table and started carving the roast chicken.

"White or dark meat?" Mom asked Allie.

"Why don't you ask Sam? She seems to know everything," Allie said, crossing her arms tight around her body.

"What's that supposed to mean?" I said.

"Girls, let's try to have a nice dinner," Mom said.

We started eating in silence. I could hear the clinking of forks and knives and the sound of chewing, which I hate. After a minute or two of clinking and chewing, Allie pointed her fork at me. "I just can't sit here with Little Miss Know-It-All and pretend it's okay that she and her boyfriend trashed the play I have been working my butt off for during the last two weeks!" At the words "Little Miss Know-It-All," my body stiffened. She couldn't have meant anything more by that, could she?

"Allie, it was just one little school newspaper review, the middle school at that, and anyway, we said you were *good*!" I cried.

"Gee, thanks, like you guys are qualified to have any opinion about the theater," Allie spit back with such anger in her face that I wanted to get up and run out of the house. I really couldn't take it anymore.

"Allie, you may be upset, and you have a right to your feelings and opinions. But so does Sam. In our house we respect one another's opinions even if they are different," Mom said.

Now Allie and I both had our arms crossed and were staring at each other, wondering who was going to make the next move. *Sisters Challenge Each Other to a Fork Duel.*

"I'm not hungry anymore," Allie said, and pushed back her plate. "May I be excused, please?"

Mom sighed. "Okay, Allie. Just clean your plate, please."

Mom and I sat there, quietly finishing our dinner.

"She'll calm down," Mom said, patting my hand. "You didn't do anything wrong, Samantha, but sometimes it stings a little when you hear the truth. She'll come around."

The next day I sat in the back of the room

with Michael at the post-issue *Voice* meeting. I was still feeling awful. Two additional people had said things to me today about the review, and they weren't compliments.

Mr. Trigg started the meeting like he always did. "Greetings, fellow journos. So our new arts reporters have stirred up quite the controversy." He grinned at me and Michael. I was in no mood for Mr. Trigg's theatrics. I'd had enough of the theater. "This is a good thing, and exactly what I meant about getting out of our comfort zones."

Really? He wanted me and Michael to basically have eggs thrown at us? That wasn't getting out of our comfort zones, that was being thrown into a war zone, I thought.

"Which is always good for us as writers and for the paper," he continued. "This is what journalism is about, folks—getting people to talk, and not being afraid to tell the truth the way we see it," he said, looking at me. "So let's talk back. Michael, Sam. There are a lot of letters to the editor about the review. What about publishing a rebuttal?"

Michael and I looked at each other. Had

Mr. Trigg lost his marbles? I just wanted this whole thing to go away.

"I don't know about that, Mr. Trigg," I said. "Won't it just make things worse?"

"We don't want to feed the fire. But I also don't think the backlash is fair. We are entitled to our opinions," Michael said.

Great, so now Michael wanted to do the rebuttal. Mr. Trigg said that professional critics do this all the time. The staff went back and forth on the issue for a while and hadn't come to a decision when the meeting time was up.

"Okay, Michael, Sam, and Susannah, we'll reconvene in a couple of days to make the final decision and see what the mood is out there. For the next issue, we'll all go back to our regular posts and see what you bring to that from your new experiences."

I breathed a sigh of relief at the thought of going back to what I did best—researching a story, not criticizing people's artistry. After all this, though, I was surprised to feel that I still stood by our review. We told it like we saw it.

Chapter 13

UNLIKELY HERO SAVES THE DAY!

"Pasty, check this out!" Michael said, running up to me in the hallway one morning a few days later, waving a copy of the local newspaper.

I glanced at what he thrust in front of me. It was a review of *West Side Story*. Michael was breathless. His eyes sparkled. Had he run all the way to school just to tell me something? I quickly scanned the review. The critic talked about the strong singing and dancing talent and the stellar history of the drama club, and she even said that "Allison Martone's exuberant and well-executed performance as Anita was a highlight." She also mentioned the unfortunate scenery and lighting mishaps—even a few more than we had cited—and had a few lines about the inconsistency of Julia Gowen's performance. But the best part was one of the last lines: "Even the middle school reviewers who came to see the play for the *Cherry Valley Voice* could see that this run was not the club's best."

"Not only did she validate our review," Michael said, poking at the article, "but we were mentioned in the local paper. How cool is that?"

"Wow," I said reading the line over again. "Well, at least now we know we weren't crazy to make the criticisms that we did." It did feel good to have a professional reviewer second our opinion and take some of the weight off our shoulders. I had always been a fan of our local paper, but now I felt like bursting through the doors of their office and giving the arts editor a hug. *Unlikely Hero Saves the Day!*

"We should go out and celebrate our celebrity!" Michael blurted out.

"Yeah, sure," I said, not really taking in what he was saying at first. I gave the paper back to him.

"What are you doing Friday after school?" he asked me.

"Um, nothing," I said, looking up in surprise.

"How about another round of pizza and ice cream?"

I smiled. "Absolutely. We definitely deserve at least a slice of pizza for our trouble," I said, and we both laughed. So, according to my guidelines, this had to qualify as a date, right?

"Great," he said. "Gotta run!"

Off he went with his backpack slung over his shoulder. In a daze, I watched him walk away until someone snapped a finger in front of my face.

"Earth to Sam," Hailey called out.

"Oh, hi!" I said, switching back to reality.

"You have that dreamy 'I just had a good conversation with Michael Lawrence' look," she said.

"How do you know me so well?" I asked her.

"Isn't that a job requirement for a best friend?" she asked.

"Yes, and you're really good at your job," I said. Hailey beamed. I told her about the local paper's review and about Michael's offer of pizza and ice cream on Friday.

"That sounds like a date to me!" she said. We would see.

The rest of the day, people were talking about

the local paper's review instead of our own, which was a huge relief. Some people were mad at the town critic now instead of at us, but others had started to agree with us and accept the fact that the play hadn't been perfect, now that a professional had given weight to our opinions.

That night at dinner, Allie complained about the local paper's review too.

"They just didn't get it," she said, shaking her head.

"But, honey, in both reviews you were the shining star," Mom said. "Doesn't that mean something?"

Allie was quiet for a moment. "Of course it does," she said, and looked at me. "It means a lot. I just feel bad for everyone else."

After dinner there was a knock at my door. "Can I come in?" asked Allie as she barged in.

I took a deep breath. *Here it comes*, I thought.

"Did you really think I was good in the play?" Allie asked.

I stared at her. "What?!"

"Well, some of the kids in the drama club said

you just gave me a good review because I was your sister."

"They what?" I sputtered. Now I was really mad.

"Well . . . did you?" Allie asked.

"Of course not!" I yelled. "I mean, if you were really bad, that would have been hard, but you were the one great thing about the play. You should have been the lead."

Allie had a big smile on her face now.

"Besides, it wasn't just us who gave you a great review either."

"That's what I told them," said Allie. "But Julia is really mad and, well, she convinced a few kids that the reviews were rigged."

"Oh for goodness' sake!" I said. "They were just reviews! This is really going too far."

"Yeah," said Allie. "It's a touchy group. But you know, I think they are all really mad because the reviews were no surprise. We all knew there were problems. We knew that the scenery crashed and that Julia wasn't terrific and that it was just too big a production. Sometimes the truth hurts."

"I'm learning that," I said. Just then I realized

that Allie had agreed with my review. "Well, all that's past us now. I'm going back to news reporting next week. So no more reviews for me."

"That's probably a good thing!" said Allie.

"Allie, in all honesty, you were great. Even if the show overall wasn't great, you were great in it."

Allie actually blushed. Then she gave me a really big smile. "Thanks, Sam. That means a lot. Well . . . good night. And . . . well, thanks for the good review. And I'm glad you're going back to writing about news before next year's show!"

"Thanks," I said, and grinned.

"Hey, just being honest," said Allie as she left my room.

That night I finally knew what to write back to Too Honest:

Dear Too Honest,

Sometimes people think they want to hear the truth, but when it's not positive, they do some serious backpedaling. Maybe your friend thought she wanted to hear your advice, but ultimately was not ready for the truth, or the truth as you saw it. Basically, advice is subjective. Beyond math and science, the way each of us sees things is only our opinion of what we think we see. It is okay for you and your friend to disagree. Because, after all, true friends should ultimately respect you for your honesty. Maybe, with a little time, they just might see it your way.

Ha! I thought as I folded the letter and put it in my bag. *That goes for sisters, too.*

Extra! Extra!

Want the scoop on what Samantha is up to next?

Here's a sneak peek of the sixth book in the Dear Know-It-All series:

Digital Disaster

MYSTERIOUS SCANDAL ROCKS SCHOOL TO THE CORE

On Monday morning at school, after a nice weekend of mostly sleeping in and watching my favorite shows I'd DVR'd but hadn't been able to watch for, like, a month, Michael came running up to me while I was trying to unstick the zipper on my black fleece jacket. Even though it was technically spring, it was still pretty cold.

"Hey, Sam, did you hear about what happened?"

I looked up from my zipper immediately. Michael called me Sam only when something was really serious. He was breathless, his face flushed.

"No?" My heart started to beat really fast. I stuffed my hands in my jacket pockets and braced myself for what he was about to tell me.

"Someone stole the math exam."

"Wait a minute, stole it? What do you mean?" I asked.

"Well, not stole it exactly. The day before the exam, the math department teachers couldn't get onto the computer system because the password had been changed. They thought an administrator or another teacher had changed it. They were able to retrieve the files, but it took them a day to figure out it was no one on the staff. It probably was a student trying to get the test ahead of time." Michael's hands moved wildly about while he was talking. He seemed upset, but also kind of excited.

"That's pretty serious," I said, but was sort of relieved. I'm just glad it wasn't about anybody getting hurt or something. "How do you even know this?" I asked.

"I saw Mr. Trigg this morning. He told me everything and wants us to do a story on it. We're going to talk about it at our meeting today."

"Wow," I said, trying to get my head around the whole thing. I wondered what it was going to mean for all of us.

I went back to my zipper. I had to be in language

arts in less than five minutes and I still had my jacket on. I tugged it down as hard as I could, but no luck.

"Let me help you there, Pasty," Michael said. Before I could respond, he grabbed the zipper and gave it a hard pull. Finally my jacket opened and there Michael was, standing there still holding the zipper. We stared at each other.

"Uh-oh," he said.

I couldn't help but laugh. "Thanks a lot, Lawrence!"

"I guess I don't know my own strength," he joked, but then he lowered his eyes and looked uncomfortable. "I'm really sorry. Can I buy you a new jacket?"

I was speechless. He was too good to be true this Michael Lawrence. "Uh." I forced myself to say something. "That's really nice to offer, but I'm sure my mom can fix it." I stuck my hand out for the zipper. "At least I don't have to wear my jacket to class, so thanks!"

He grinned. "No problem. Anytime you need your clothes ruined, you know who to call."

I laughed and he handed me back my zipper. I

couldn't wait to tell Hailey about this, and I couldn't help but wonder what he would have done if I'd taken him up on the new jacket offer. Would we have gone shopping together? Maybe I had just made a big mistake turning him down. After I put my broken jacket in my locker, Michael and I walked together to class. His seat was right in front and I was in the middle. We sat down. The room was buzzing. Everyone all around me was already discussing the big news. How had people found out so fast? Mr. Farrell, our teacher, was trying to get the class's attention by turning the lights on and off. It took a while for people to settle down. ***Mysterious Scandal Rocks School to the Core.***

I wondered who was stupid enough to do something like this, if that was the case. The truth was, no one knew what had actually happened. But if it was a student, had he done it because he was really afraid he'd do badly on the test, or had he just wanted to cause some major drama? I looked around. It could have been anyone, maybe even someone right in this room!

If you like **DEAR** KNOW-IT-ALL

books, then you'll love

SARANORMAL

EBOOK EDITIONS ALSO AVAILABLE

Published by Simon Spotlight • KIDS.SimonandSchuster.com